The Best Friend & The Shortstop

GINGER SCOTT

For love of the game.

prologue

Freshman Year, Tiff University

nikki thomas

IF ALEX TELLS me to relax one more time, I'm going to punch him in the crotch. First college party is a big deal for me. My best friend has been sneaking out and slipping into parties at the Tiff frat houses for two years now. It's different for guys. Double standards somehow make it cool to be too young to be here when you have a dick. The one time I tried to come with Alex I was stamped with a huge sticker that read UNDERAGE. He, however, was allowed to play the part of twenty-one all night long.

No stickers for me this time, though. I might only be eighteen, but I'm a real Tiff student, so bent rules finally apply to me. And it's the fact all of this—*the college experience*—is real that has me nervous and fidgety.

"Don't you want to blend in? Or are you trying to make a name for yourself as the girl who can't stop pulling her skirt down, adjusting her shirt, touching her hair, or whatever other movement you're about to do?"

His phrasing catches me with my hand an inch away from my eyelashes. I was on my way to double check they were still there, which, yes, I relent . . . it's a little neurotic. Of course they're there. I'd see them fall off—being that they're glued atop my eyeballs and all that.

I swing my right arm out and smack Alex dead center in the chest.

"Ooof!" He grabs my wrist and clutches it as he hunches over from my blow.

"Cheap shot, Nik. Cheap. Shot."

I jerk my hand away and grimace.

"Cheap would have been lifting a knee." I bring my leg up but stop a few inches from his balls. His eyes flash wide and he flinches his body away, cupping himself.

"Whoa, okay. I'll lay off. It's just . . . you're going to be fine. Whatever you've built this whole party thing into in your head"—he taps the side of my skull, and I fight the urge to flinch or check whether he messed up my tightly pulled ponytail—"It's probably going to disappoint you. Because the version of college parties you see in the movies? That's BS, Nik. Mostly, these things are broken down by a bunch of people smoking pot by a pool that may or may not have water in it while a bunch of *other* people grind against each other in a living room furnished with hand-me-downs and Goodwill finds. And then there's the people who never come downstairs because they're too old for this shit, so they stay up in their rooms . . . probably smoking pot or grinding on someone."

My mouth goes flat and I blink at him. I know he's trying to make the college scene seem a lot like the high school parties we went to back home, but there's one major difference I can't get over. For all intents and purposes, we're all considered *adults*.

Granted, the whole drinking thing still has rules, but even that is different when a parent isn't waiting at home to smell your breath. The fact is, nobody is waiting at home, no curfew, no worried dad constantly checking the front window. And I *know* Alex has a condom in his wallet that he plans on using sometime tonight, which . . . I wish I didn't know about.

Strange shivers start at my neck and dart down my spine, so I cut that thought off before it takes over and simply nod a promise that I'll try to relax.

It's easier to play along. To let him play the too-familiar part of surrogate big brother. It's what he's always done. It's how he sees me, still. After all these years. This gap between us only widened the moment he grasped that high school diploma in his hands. Cute Alex gave way to something more mature. He started to look like a man and not the boy with noodle arms who I kept pitch count for in junior high and high school. He grew his hair a little longer. His jaw cut sharper and his forearms got these waves caused by tendons and burgeoning muscles. His shoulders bulked up, and his back got wider. And his thighs—*good God, his thighs!*

Alex Mendoza has always had the perfect smile framed by adorable dimples. That winning grin got our asses out of a lot of trouble when my abuela watched us after school. It got him a lot of girlfriends in high school, too. And over the years, it did quite a number on me. The number of times I practiced writing my first name with his last in notebooks is too embarrassing to ever let anyone, let alone Alex, see. *Thank God we had a fireplace! I burned every one of those notes.*

Alex was my first crush. At first, for all the reasons he was my best friend: he's kind, funny, playful, brave. Things really amped up, though, after we all went to the lake after graduation and he burst up through the water's surface all golden-skinned, ripped as hell, and smiling. Those dimples, paired with his dark, wet hair that he shook out then smoothed back with one hand, had me sunk. And I haven't been able to climb back to the surface since.

Three months of seeing my best friend with totally new eyes. And fantasizing about him in extremely unfriendly ways thanks to one *very* graphic dream the night after the lake. It's made hanging out together weird, but probably only for me. I don't think Alex underwent the same *aha* moment I did. I'm still waiting on my *glow up*. And I fear forcing it out with these fake eyelashes was a huge mistake. These things are miserable.

"Hi, freshmen! Welcome to Sigma!" Without warning, a blonde wearing five-inch heels with straps that wrap up her calves drops a fake floral lei over my head. The blossoms are bright yellow, and I'm about to request a trade for the pink one dangling from her palm when her attention instantly diverts to Alex.

"I'm Tiara. And *you* are going to come with me for drinks," she says, looping the pink lei over Alex's head and proceeding to lead him by it toward a keg propped at a table in what I guess is the dining room.

Tiara. As in royal headwear?

"I guess we're getting beer," Alex says through a chuckle over his shoulder. Damn him, even his naïve shrug is cute.

"*Hmm*, I guess so."

I begrudgingly trail behind them, my heavy brow in full-sulk mode. It took four minutes for me to become a third wheel.

I follow Tinkerbell and my best friend to the keg, and when Alex hands me a full cup, I smirk at him over the rim before tipping it back and taking a big drink.

"What's that look for?" he says, playing coy.

I shake my head as I pull the cup from my lips, my puckered smile barely holding in my usual acerbic zinger.

"Nothing at all. Absolutely nothing. No look here. All in your imagination." I let the tight-lipped smile rest as I hold his gaze, and his eyes dim briefly before he rolls them and turns back to the keg to fill his own cup.

"I just wonder if there will be a coronation," I say, leaning in. He drops his chin to his chest and puffs out a short laugh. I can't see his eyes, but I know they're closed. He's also probably smiling because as snarky as I am, I'm also funny. Nobody makes him laugh like I do. Especially girls named *Tiara*.

"Perhaps a knighting ceremony. *Ooooh!* Will you give her a favor? Will there be jousting?" It's too late to stop the flood from my mouth. It's one of my flaws, but knowing it's a flaw is only half the battle. I have time to work on keeping it in check later. Besides, Tiara is talking to an older guy near the keg. Seems she's already cut Alex loose. *Or maybe she simply added him to her collection.*

Alex stands tall and stares at me over his cup as he takes a slow sip. I shrug, my non-verbal version of, "What?"

"You're a real dick sometimes, you know that?" he says.

Our banter has always been like this. Buddies. Bros. Familiar. Yet my cheeks are hot and I swear I can feel the prickling of tears in the corners of my eyes. His words have never burned in my chest before. But right now? I'm on fire.

"Sorry," I mutter, glancing away and turning my body along with my gaze. I blink rapidly, regretting the stupid eyelashes and wishing I wore my ripped-up jeans and Toxic Pillows tour shirt instead of this scooped-neck top that barely covers my midriff and chest at the same time.

I reach down with my free hand and tug my skirt lower a half-second before Alex's hand covers mine. My eyes dart up to his. He's standing close. It's loud in here, but I swear I can't hear a thing beyond the thumping of my heart. I'm not supposed to react this way. The thousands of times we've touched hands—hell, slept next to each other in a tent or on the living room floor, for that matter —touching shouldn't affect me like this.

He squeezes my fingers in his palm, and everything becomes . . . *more.*

"I didn't mean it." He blinks a few times, but his gaze sticks to mine. Somehow, the burning in my chest has changed. It's still hot, but it also vibrates with what feels like electricity. A touch of terror. But mostly electricity.

"I know." My voice is as close to a whisper as I can get it yet still be heard.

Alex shakes my hand softly then lets go, my fingers flexing with an instant hunger to be grasped again. My hand is cold. My neck is cold. *I'm* cold. Alex took one step back and his eyes left me, and that's all it took for me to feel his departure.

I have to keep swimming. If I don't, I'll drown like this.

"Come on," he says, nodding toward the open living room where two guys seem to be arguing over who gets to put the next song in the queue on the computer. Judging by the rancid noise nearly busting the speaker, my vote is for neither of them.

"You should probably introduce yourself," Alex says, nudging me toward the wannabe-DJs. I give him side eyes, and a playful smirk tickles the side of my mouth.

"Go on. You know you're dying to take over."

"I am," I laugh out softly before leaving my best friend to the already full sectional sofa filled with his future female fans. They gobble him up like piranhas the second he sinks into the corner seat.

Alex came to Tiff on a full ride to play baseball. He'll likely be one of the first freshmen to start at shortstop for Tiff since his dad did twenty-six years ago. He's bound for the big leagues, assuming he wants them. His dad didn't, which is something Alex has wrestled with for years. I think he blames himself—more specifically, his birth. I believe his dad chose a family life because it's what he wanted. Alex has always struggled with the idea that anything could be better than being in the game. It's where his heart beats strongest. Anyone watching him play can see it.

It's beautiful.

And the coeds fighting over who sits next to him right now are going to have bona fide wars for his attention when fall ball starts up in a month.

"Vipers," I mutter to myself. I roll my shoulders and do my best to shake off the tinge of jealousy before introducing myself to the two guys working the computer.

"Hey, I'm Nikki. Mind if I . . ." I flash a crooked smile and lift a shoulder, and their gazes dart down to my cleavage.

"Right, so that's a yes. Excuse me." I step in front of the taller one with unkempt curly hair. He smells of cotton candy and spearmint, the new college cologne thanks to an abundance of vape stores near campus.

"Just keep it chill," his friend advises me, his breath somehow leaving condensation on my neck. *Gross.*

"I got it," I say, *snarky Nikki* making an appearance.

He reacts with the probably appropriate *okay* as he holds up his hands. Alex's words immediately echo in my mind.

You're a real dick sometimes.

I'm not sure that applies when guys like this breathe way too close and ogle my tits, but perhaps I snapped too soon.

"And no chick music," he adds, reaffirming my initial summation.

I don't even bother looking at him this time. But I do let his misogyny and general douchey-ness inspire the mix I build. Most people don't know how to use these music apps to their full capability, but you spend enough time hiding behind mixers and messing around loading your dad's old albums into digital and you pick up a thing or two. In about five minutes, I've built a steady R&B beat that will carry on for the next thirty minutes, rotating through mixes made of Taylor Swift hits, Pink, and, because I really love the old-school stuff, Tina Turner.

"That *dude* enough for you?" I pat the chatty one on the chest and push past his curly-haired friend, wedging my way next to my best friend on the sofa.

"This is good," he says, pointing up to compliment the sound.

"I know." I shrug.

A soft laugh slips from his lips, private, just for me. I relish it for a second before my gaze expands to take in the crowd around him that seems to have doubled. All females. Well, *almost* all. One guy is sitting on the sofa arm. He's a little bulkier than Alex, with dirty blond hair, a mustache, and stubble. Clearly a teammate—he's dressed head to toe in Tiff baseball wear.

"Hey," I say, reaching across Alex's chest to introduce myself. The guy's eyes peel away from the girl sitting behind me and meet mine. His smile is nice. "I'm Nikki."

"Nice to meet you, Nikki. I'm Brayden. You . . . with Alex?" Brayden's finger swirls at the space between me and my friend.

"Ha! No, she's like my sister," Alex answers quickly.

I laugh along with him, maybe a little harder just to lay it on thick. *Alex and me? Nah, that would be crazy! Right?* My insides tighten the way they do on terrifying roller coasters at the state fair.

"Sorry, I just thought—"

"Wait, so you two . . . you're not together?" the girl next to me asks, scooting in close and leaning over my lap, the tips of her long brown hair tickling the tops of my bare thighs.

"No, we are not together," I say matter-of-factly. I flick her hair away and she sits back again, huffing out a short laugh.

"Why is that funny?" Alex's tone isn't as irritated as mine. Probably because he doesn't find this irritating. Hurtful. Hopeless.

"You guys . . . I don't know, *look* like a couple," the girl says.

"Yeah, that's what I thought, too. Like, you guys have a

vibe or whatever," Brayden adds. My gaze darts to him, and I can feel my mouth contort with confusion. I'm sure my expression looks like disgust, but it's far from that. It's more like panic that other people see the way I look at Alex and have construed it into a vibe. I'm a step away from being the sad former bestie with an unrequited crush.

"Pssshh, vibe." I glance at Alex, expecting the same amused expression I'm forcing on my face, but instead, he almost seems intrigued by the idea.

"Our moms are best friends. We basically grew up together," Alex explains, his eyes dancing over me with what feels like a sense of fondness. Maybe I simply want that to be the case. Years of play dates, slumber parties, field trips, getting grounded together, sneaking out while grounded. Our stories are intertwined. One.

"You never fooled around? Like, parents weren't home so you made out or anything like that?" the girl asks.

"Ha, no! Make out," I say, following it up with a snort-laugh like I'm eleven and embarrassed by kissing talk. My skin is hot, though, so I may be a little embarrassed. Mostly, I feel like everyone can see right through me all of a sudden.

"You should kiss now. I mean, to know for sure. Don't you think?" The girl, our instigator, sits up and tucks a leg under her body to prop herself up higher and collect more attention. My hands are pouring sweat. I rub them down my skirt then onto my bare thighs, letting my skin stick to itself.

"I don't think we need to test that," Alex laughs off.

"Yeah, I mean . . ." I look around without focusing on a single face staring back at me. I can't seem to find the off switch for my nervous laugh.

"It's college. Kissing isn't a big deal. I do it all the time," she says, promptly standing and walking over to Alex. Within a breath, she's on her knees and tugging the collar of this black T-shirt into her. I catch my friend's eyes as his gaze hits mine with a brief, panicked wideness about a half second before they close and the girl's lips are on his. Her hands snake up his jaw, the sharp tips of her ice blue nails scratching his skin as their heads shift and mouths open. The rage borne of my jealousy boils to a flash point, and my worst instincts take over.

"I mean, yeah. I can do that! Anyone can do that," I say, prompting her to pull away with a smirk just after her teeth pull at his bottom lip before parting.

Shit. I'm not sure I can kiss like that.

"Go on then. Assuming you're game for this?" She quirks a brow to Alex, who seems unable to form words. The stupid open-mouthed smile on his face and bashful laugh that bubbles from his chest is all we're going to get.

"I'm Alicia, by the way," she says, taking his hand and stepping to the side, presumably to give me her coveted position. *On my knees in front of Alex.*

"Alex," my friend manages to utter to his kissing buddy, his damn flirtatious dimples making an appearance. He looks drunk already. Half a beer in. *Stupid male libido.*

I place my hands on his knees as I kneel in front of him, drawing his attention to me. He licks his bottom lip, his smile shifting into a timid one. This is not how my first kiss with Alex was supposed to go. And though I only just met Alicia, I hate her for putting me in this spot. Mostly, I hate that I'm letting her. That I want to kiss Alex so much that I'm willing to use this ridiculous pretense simply to have the chance. That I'm watering down my feelings and possibly ruining any hope for a future *us*.

Or maybe . . . maybe he'll feel something, too.

I lick my lips as I adjust my balance on my knees and scoot in closer. Alex breathes out a short laugh, his lips puckering the way they do when he's holding in serious laughter. The sense that he finds this funny sits heavy in my chest.

"Well?" Alex tilts his head. His eyes lock on mine, pupils dilating as he relaxes and parts his lips. The smirk is still there, playing at the right side, inching upward to make the dimple.

I lean in and close my eyes, hoping he'll meet me halfway. I'm not sure whether everyone's holding their breath or I've lost my hearing. Either way, it's complete silence in our tiny bubble. Alex's hand cups my right cheek, fingertips gliding through my hairline as a tiny breath leaves my lips. The electricity touches my lips first, followed by the warm, soft fullness of his mouth against mine. Time may have slowed, but regardless, I firmly believe he isn't rushing this. I know I'm not. I lean in, boldly clutching the front of his shirt as he sucks in my bottom lip, his tongue grazing it. A soft whimper is trapped in my throat and I let it out, hoping it's both loud enough for Alex to hear and soft enough for our audience to not.

Alex's hand fades away from my skin, his fingertips lingering under my chin as his lips leave mine. I exhale softly and blink my eyes open in time to witness Alex doing the same. For a beat, our eyes lock, and I would swear on my soul—on *his* soul—that he felt something in our kiss. If we were alone, I'd challenge him and insist he prove otherwise if he didn't admit it. But we're not alone. And Alicia claps her hands together once with the force of a third-grade teacher attempting to wrangle students hyped on sugar. Her sharp interruption bursts our bubble, breaking our gaze.

"Well? How was it?" She slips into the space next to Alex, where I was sitting. My space.

"It was . . . I don't know . . ." Alex glances at me, and I can't tell whether he's waiting for me to answer or if he's searching for the right words. His brow draws in, almost as if he's searching, then his shoulders rise. "Weird, I guess?"

Weird. Not magical. Not even interesting. Hell, *strange* would have been better. But weird? *He said weird.*

"Huh. I guess you guys were right." Alicia sums up our experience without even asking me what I think. I don't dispute it, though, because my God, how embarrassing would that be? Instead, I chuckle through the utter despair settling into my chest cavity. I mutter, "Yeah, weird," the room no longer interested.

A few minutes pass and the conversation shifts. I make my way back to the computer where my playlist is still going strong and drown myself in a folder titled VINTAGE 70s. And after an hour of showing my tricks to the two hopeless music geeks who let me horn in on their space, I spot Alex linking hands with Alicia and heading up the stairs.

nikki thomas, senior year

MY EYES CONNECT with Alex's over the roof of his car just as my mom rushes from the garage with one more bag of nearly-expired baked goods she picked up from the clearance bakery. At first, our friends at Tiff didn't believe us when we told them the clearance bakery was a thing. But now that we've consistently come back from Odell, our hometown about three hours north of Tiff, with sacks upon sacks of baked goods, they've all bought into the truth. The problem is they encourage our moms' obsession. Mostly because we return to campus with treats every time we go home.

"I knew I had one more. Here, Nik. You can put it on the floor." My mom hooks the bag on my finger then plops a quick kiss on my cheek before running back into the garage and shutting it behind her.

"Remind me again why we came home for a three-day weekend?" I peek inside the bag as I slump into the passenger seat.

"Because if we didn't come here, they would come to us," Alex reminds me, his eyes crinkling in that sweet way that accompanies his smile.

"Ah," I respond, pulling out the box of last-chance powdered donuts and cracking the lid. "Well, we better eat these on the road. They expire tomorrow."

I pluck one out and take a bite. Alex nudges the box lid down, scanning it with his eyes, and laughs.

"They expired two days ago," he says, and I cough out a fog of powdered sugar. Flipping the box lid back open, he nods for me to dispose of the remains. I power through chewing what I already ate, my mind working through the psychology of whether I realized the donut was stale before or after I knew the date.

We both buckle up for the drive. I turn my attention to syncing my phone with his car so I can continue testing my mixes on him—*and* avoiding the conversation I promised my friend Omar I would have. I made a deal for the last piece of cheesecake at our resident hall staff meeting last week that during this trip with Alex, I would finally let him know how I feel. Seeing as I have a couple hours and a few hundred miles left in the trip, I think I might owe Omar cheesecake.

I start the next song in the queue and am about to explain my thought process on the songs I chose when Alex halts me with a sharp laugh. My brow draws in tight.

"What?" My hand immediately goes to the corners of my mouth, feeling the sugar.

"Hold on. You're making it worse." Alex twists in his

seat and cradles my face in his palms, his thumbs smudging away what probably looks like cocaine or paste by this point from both sides of my mouth. I'd be embarrassed if I weren't busy relishing this moment.

I wonder if he can hear my heartbeat.

"Better?" I ask, my own breath fighting against self-control. How is it I feel as if I just finished sprinting a forty? I should be better at suppressing my physical reaction to him by now. Years of practice and all that. But the fact that finally confessing how I feel to him has been balancing on the edge of my lips all weekend is making it hard.

"Yeah. I got you," Alex says, snapping me from my haze. He winks as his hands drop from my face. They're back on the wheel a half second later and we're on our way back toward campus.

I settle into my seat and tie the last-minute bakery bag into a knot at the top and drop it at my feet. I'm sure one of Alex's teammates won't care that the donuts are stale. Or that I ate half of one.

Forcing myself to refocus, I restart the music. I'm applying for an apprenticeship with a sound studio after graduation, mostly to build my portfolio before attempting to branch out on my own. I want to own my own studio, work with female indie artists, maybe run the sound for a tour one day. I've spent three and a half years in Tiff's broadcasting school making connections and nerding out with sound engineers, but the experience has all been with sports. It's time for me to turn my passion for music into a career. My portfolio needs to show more than my work for play-by-play and commercial breaks. That's why I made these mixes as a supplement. I was hoping Alex could help me narrow down the best two or three to include.

The beat thumps through the sub in Alex's trunk, rattling some of the boxes our moms sent with us back to campus. I lean on the console to mess with the bass levels, though I'd prefer to mess with the boxes instead. I find a happy medium and am about to launch back into my thought process for slowing down a classic disco refrain when Alex speaks.

"I know we need to get back, but mind stopping at the high school?"

I snap my mouth shut and consider the clues in his words. Alex Sr. is there, at the field, working out the high school team for pre-season. I noticed Alex didn't visit practice all weekend. In fact, he hasn't stopped by the school to see the team or help out his dad since he left for summer ball before our senior year at Tiff. And he spent more time at our house than his over winter break last month. Same with this weekend trip. His relationship with his dad has always been hard to pin down. I figure when your dad is both your idol and your coach, things get strained. I was there for the tough rides home after bad games. And his dad was always extra hard on him, partly to avoid showing favoritism. But also, I think there was a part of him that rose or fell depending on his son's successes and failures. Alex shuts me down when I bring up this new level of tension, insisting everything is the same. He forgets that I'm one of the few people in his life who recognizes when it's not.

"Of course," I answer, my gaze lingering on his. He seems hesitant, as if he wants to change his mind. Eventually, though, he nods and moves his focus to the rearview mirror before shifting into reverse. I settle into my seat and buckle up.

We're at the school in minutes. Alex pulls along the fence, parking under the tree he and I used to climb up in when we were young to watch his dad coach. I unclasp my safety belt and put my hand on the door.

"I'll only be a minute," he says, leaving the engine running.

"Oh, okay," I say, quietly clicking my seat belt back in place.

I pause my mix, figuring I'll start it over when we hit the road for real. Plus, I'm hoping I'll be able to hear something if I crack the window. Alex's dad says something to one of his players then walks around the dugout to meet his son. They're too far for me to eavesdrop, but I do my best to read the body language. There isn't a handshake. The two men haven't hugged in years. Their stances are similar, however, both nodding with their arms folded over their chests, eyes peering down at the ground between them.

As promised, Alex is heading back to the car in less than a minute. Whatever their conversation, it was brief.

"Thanks," Alex says, slipping back into the driver's

seat as if he merely stepped out to wash the windshield. I stare at him as he snaps his belt back in place and shifts into drive. He relents and meets my gaze after a few long seconds.

"It's fine. We're . . . fine." Nothing about his tone sounds fine.

He flexes his hands on the steering wheel. I shift my gaze out my window and chew the inside of my mouth to keep from needling him. The quiet feels thick, though, and I don't want to simply replace it with my music.

"Good thing he's not your coach anymore, I guess." It's a bit passive aggressive, but it's also not a direct question, and Alex relents with a sighed laugh.

"I asked him not to come to my games is all. For a while, at least."

My eyebrows have always betrayed me, and I feel them touch my hairline when Alex looks at me.

"For a while, I said," he repeats, a little snap to his retort.

"Yeah, I heard you the first time," I throw back. He doesn't have to tell me what's going on between him and his dad if he doesn't want to, but he does have to redirect his bad mood. I'm definitely not revealing my years-long crush to him now. Hell, if he keeps this attitude up I may just quash my feelings for good.

Probably not.

I let the silence grow, waiting him out. I know him well enough to realize he hopes I'll just drop this subject and get lost in sharing my work with him. Normally, I would.

But this feels serious. He finally breaks, rolling his head and grabbing the back of his neck as he sighs.

"I haven't been hitting great in scrimmages. And there's this freshman—"

"Edwin," I fill in, knowing who he means. Because I've watched the scrimmages. And he's right, he hasn't been hitting great. And Edwin has. But Alex has three years of evidence for what he can do in the batter's box. He shouldn't let a few rough weeks of fall ball eat away at him. Which is easy for me to say, I suppose.

"Yeah. Anyway, he's probably going to get to DH a lot to start, and if I can't turn it around . . ."

I swivel my head in time to see him swallow hard. He glances my way briefly but returns his focus to the road.

"I don't know. It's just got me thinking about distractions is all. And *he's* one hell of a distraction." Our eyes meet for a second and he flashes me a quick, guilty half-smirk.

"I understand."

His mouth is pulled into a tight line. He's grinding his teeth. I recognize the ripples along his jawline. I place my hand on his forearm and his gaze shifts to me again. He lets go of the wheel and links our hands, squeezing my palm in his. It's warm and safe. Like always.

"Thanks," he says, letting go of his hold and returning his hands to the ever-so-safe ten and two.

I leave the obvious things off to the side, like the fact his dad really is proud of his son. Whatever this strife is, I doubt it has to do with him wanting his father's approval or attention. If anything, he's always wanted a little less of it.

"Sorry, I didn't mean to suck the air out of the car. You were about to explain why I should like this hot take on your dad's record collection." He turns the music up as he cracks a joke, his way of changing subjects.

"Right." I exhale. "So, first off, this phrase is from a Diana Ross song. And it's *my* record, thank you very much." Alex relaxes into a soft laugh. I continue, my mind splitting into two different paths. There's my present, here in the car, continuing to talk about my passion with my friend, and then there's the other me, drifting down the rabbit hole of worries for my friend, and owning that I won't be admitting my feelings to him anytime soon. Also, I need to stop for cheesecake.

I'M NOT sure what clued Omar in first, the fact that he opened the door to my scrunched-up, guilty expression or the box of frozen cheesecake I clutched in my hands. Perhaps it was both pieces of evidence together. Regardless, here we are on the floor of his resident assistant room with a couple of forks, frosty raspberry-topped cheesecake, and box wine that we are drinking right from the spout.

"I hear what you're saying, Nikki. I wouldn't have wanted to talk about my crush on that drive home either," Omar says, sliding his fork into a piece of the cake.

"Good, you understand then. Thank you," I say, piercing my next bite.

"Ah, but . . ." He cups his mouth to chew and talk at the same time.

I don't bother taking my bite. Here comes my lecture.

"You *did* have the entire weekend. And, as you mentioned, Alex was at your house basically the entire time." He quirks a brow as he swallows his bite and drops his hand from masking his righteous grin.

"No more cheesecake for you," I say, slapping the lid back on our treat and getting to my feet. I'm a little tipsy from the cheap wine and manage to stumble back a step but quickly right myself.

Omar gets up and sucks the last remnants of cake from his fork before tossing it in the trash.

"That's fine. I'm watching my figure," he jokes, patting his extremely taut stomach. I give him side eyes and murmur, "Asshole" under my breath. He chuckles.

Omar and I have been friends for two years, since we both applied to be RAs and went through the training together, which isn't much more than CPR, first aid, and a lecture on reminding students not to have open flames in their rooms. He's a nursing major, and the most eligible gay man on Tiff's campus. He is also terrified of rejection since a bad breakup freshman year, so while he has plenty of advice for me on the dating front, he's no better at taking leaps of faith than I am.

"What if I make you a deal?" I say, sliding the cheese-cake box into the only open space in Omar's mini fridge.

"I like deals. I mean, this last one got me free cheese-cake, so . . ." He opens his palms and smirks. I grimace.

"Okay, Mr. Know-It-All." I might be a little more than just tipsy. But that's fine. My point will still be made.

"If I spill my guts to Alex, you have to ask out that lacrosse player I know you have been pining after at the gym." I cross my arms over my chest and jut out my hip, proud of my new little *all-in* gamble.

Omar chews at the inside of his cheek, the nervous side of him making his eyes flinch a tick. "*Pining* after?"

"Oh, whatever! I was trying to be classy about it, but fine—lusting after. And don't you deny it!" I point a finger at him and I swear his cheeks are pink.

"Oh, I'm not denying it. I just think I'm more up for this than you are," he challenges back, running a hand through his curly black hair. His gaze settles on mine, waiting for my next move.

I pull my phone from the back pocket of my jeans to check the time, chewing on my tongue while I consider the opportunity. It's probably halftime for the playoff basketball game going on in the gym right now, and most of our school's athletes are there supporting. Alex is, and I'd bet Brian, the hot lacrosse guy, is too. My skin buzzes with nervous energy, but if I don't do this now, I will only sober up and put it off for, well, probably forever.

"Fine. Let's see who's up for it. We're going to the

game. Get your shoes on." I kick his sneakers toward him while I sink my phone back into my pocket.

Omar drops his chin to his chest, staring at his shoes for a few seconds before shaking with a silent laugh.

"Alright, you're on, Nik. I hope you're ready." He slips one foot into a shoe, then bends down to pull the heel back for the second.

I swallow hard when he's not looking, the weight of my gauntlet hitting me. My skin is hot, which is partly from the wine, but also from panic. *Shit! I'm doing this.*

While Omar brushes his teeth, I grab a water bottle from his fridge and swish to rinse out my mouth, then crowd in next to him to spit it out in his sink. I tug the tie from my hair and run my fingers through it a few times to work out the kink. I look like I've been drinking box wine in a dorm room for the last hour so I splash water on my face and pat my skin dry with a towel, then pile my hair back up on top of my head in a cute messy bun. At least, I think it's cute. I'm not sure my opinion can be trusted right now.

"Let's do this," Omar says, holding the door open for me.

"Let's," I agree, giving him a hard brush against the chest as I pass him and head into the hall. It's bravado, but faking it has gotten me through tough spots before. Most of my successful job interviews were for things I wasn't qualified for but went in bold. I had zero soundboard experience when I applied for the Tiff broadcast truck. Now I run that thing.

Our dorm attaches to the gym through a tunnel, a convenient feature when it's snowing outside, but less so when one is hoping for this trip to take more time. We're standing in front of the crowded stands in minutes, and my pits are dripping with sweat. Omar, however, seems cool as can be.

"You find your guy?" I say, stepping up on my toes and shouting toward his ear. It's roaring in here, the game tight and our girls having just scored on a fast break. Omar scans the seats for a few seconds while I do the same.

"Got him," he finally says, nodding up toward the right hand corner where a few of the lacrosse players have gathered. "You?"

I spot Alex almost instantly. I've always been able to find him in crowds. I pretend, though, panning over the stands until acting as though I just found him. "Ah, yes. In the very middle. Of course."

Of course. Right in the middle of everyone.

My legs are trembling, and the thought that I might biff it on my way up the stands doesn't feel so far-fetched.

"Alright. It's on," Omar says, holding out his palm for me to shake. I grasp his hand and we both nod. He turns and heads up the stands to his target. I guess that makes this an official deal. Or maybe not. Maybe I walk up there and sit next to Alex and relish in the fact I did my friend Omar a solid and got him to take a shot at romance.

It's too loud in here for me to call an audible, and I stand out by hovering in front of the people seated courtside. With a massive deep breath, I ball my fists in my front pockets and focus on putting one foot in front of the other until I'm a few steps from Alex's row. We make eye contact and he nods for me to shimmy over the long legs of his teammates to take the spot next to him.

"Excuse me," I say, not realizing that the first set of legs I need to navigate past belong to my ex, Brayden.

"Not even going to stop to say hi?" He was always overly charming to the point of cheesy. It's why I wasn't so upset when we broke up. Not that I should have been dating him to begin with. It was our freshman year, and I was pissed off that Alex was spending so much time hooking up with Alicia that I tried to redirect my affection to Brayden. It was a major fail. And not only because I wasn't really invested in our relationship. Brayden's a pitcher, which comes with a certain level of narcissism. While he was dating me, he was also very much dating himself. In fact, I think he prefers himself over just about anyone. Even now, I'm guessing.

"Oh, sorry. I wasn't really paying attention. But yes, hi, Brayden. Good to see you," I say, accepting his gesture for a hug. His long arms wrap around me and I feel smothered. My gaze strains to make eye contact with Alex, and our eyes meet.

"One second," I mouth. Alex gives me a quick nod, his eyes squinting a little. Does he not like that I'm hugging Brayden? Maybe this confession mission will work out after all.

"I should . . ." I start, nodding down the line toward Alex.

"Oh, yeah. Hey, let's catch up sometime," he says, letting his hands drop back into his pockets. I nod and smile while my inner voice explains that we just did catch up and that's enough.

I work my way through the tight space over a few more sets of knees and thighs until I'm able to flop down into the space next to Alex.

"You get Omar his cheesecake?" my friend asks.

I breathe out a short laugh and nod with tight lips. He thinks I lost a bet over some residence hall survey.

"I may have had a little myself." I shrug with one shoulder, giving him a guilty smirk.

Alex leans in and lowers his brow, and my chest and neck fire up.

"You have a little something else with your dessert?" His brow ticks up on one side.

Shit. I should have snagged some mouthwash from Omar.

I hold up my fingers in a pinch.

"A little wine, maybe." *A lot of wine, probably.*

Alex chuckles, his body vibrating with his laughter against my side. At least being this close helps me avoid direct eye contact and hopefully blocks his view of my flushed skin. I might be buzzed, but my cheeks are pink for a whole different reason.

"Hey, can we talk—"

"I wanted to tell you something I've been feeling—"

We talk over one another, something we've done for

years, but the timing feels less amusing now. We both laugh nervously and insist the other person goes first, but of course, there's no way I'm dropping my truth bomb before he says what he needs to say.

"Don't make me pinch your nipple," I threaten, getting a snort-laugh from his teammate Cole on the other side of him. "Hush your mouth or I pinch yours too!" I press my thumb and index finger together and twist to emphasize my threat, but Cole simply waggles his brows and asks if I promise.

I roll my eyes and block my view of Cole behind Alex's bicep.

"I'll go first just to avoid having to watch Cole get off on letting you pinch his nipples," Alex chuckles. I shove his side, my movement a little bit playful and a little irritable at the same time. This whole thing is going badly.

Alex's body lifts with an inhale and I find myself joining him. When he exhales, however, I hold my breath in, waiting.

"About today, at the school. The whole thing with *my dad.*" He exaggerates his last two words in that sarcastic tone he uses when he's uncomfortable. I slowly release my breath through my nose. This is an important share for him. I wish it wasn't happening here, but I've prodded him over it for too long to ask him to wait.

"Yeah," I hum, leaning into him so he can feel my weight, my comfort. It's so crowded in here it almost feels intimate. No one would be able to hear us without physically leaning in. And I'm definitely buzzed enough to throat punch one of his teammates.

"Last summer, before I left for the summer league, I found out some pretty shitty stuff . . . about my dad." His chin tucks to his shoulder and his eyes drop to meet mine. My stomach sinks with worry and I gulp the air. His dad is sick.

"Oh, Alex." I instinctively wrap my hand around his forearm.

"No, not . . . not what you're thinking," he stops me. His hand covers mine, and I dissolve into my surroundings, my ears full, my heart pounding. I'm a mixed bag of emotions, but above it all I have to force myself to be present for my friend.

"My parents are separated. My mom . . . she doesn't want anyone to know, though. Because you know how our town is."

I suck in a sharp breath and nod. Odell is big enough to have the kind of people who love to spread rumors. And his mom, Marie, is a teacher at the high school where his dad is a coach. And they exist together, day in, day out. Still. *Oh, man.*

I nod.

"Does my mom know?" She can't possibly. She's terrible at keeping secrets from me, and Alex shakes his head, confirming my hunch.

"I'm impressed she's been able to keep it from her," Alex laughs out in a short breath. I flash a short-lived smile in agreement. This might be the first time one of them has kept a secret from the other, at least as far as I know.

"Is there a reason Marie hasn't told my mom?" I can't help but dig. There has to be more to it. A reason why Alex hasn't told me until now.

Alex's gaze flickers up, and he laughs. He pulls his hat from his head and runs his fingers through his hair before nestling it back in place. He gives a quick glance to his right then meets my stare.

"Remember Miss Arendale? The sub?" His eyes study me while I mentally jog through the few times I had her as a substitute in high school PE. She was nice. Young. Very attractive. She graduated from Odell High when we were freshmen, so it was a big deal to have a former student there to teach us. Especially since she was so young.

Oh.

"No!" I growl, my mouth hanging open in disbelief.

"Uh, very much yes. And guess who got a full-time gig at the school? And who is still dating, if that's what you can call it?"

My mouth somehow finds a way to fall open wider.

"Yeah, it's as bad as you imagine." His mouth snaps shut and his faint, tight smile is the indignant kind.

"And nobody knows?" A love triangle like this is a pretty big piece of gossip for Odell High. I doubt there isn't someone who's picked up on things, especially if they're still . . . *dating.* And when did it start? Was she . . . his student?

Oh, my God!

"I'm sure some of the students know," Alex says. "I wasn't exactly nice to my dad when we chatted on the field. Some of the guys heard us." He shrugs, almost as though he doesn't care that he broke the news to the public. Except, I know he cares about his mom's feelings in all of this.

"I see how he's a distraction," I say, leaning into him again to show my support.

"Yeah," he sighs. "I've been processing it all. I guess I'm *still* processing. I'm sorry I was so shitty toward you. And that I didn't tell you sooner. I've been trying to keep it separate from the good things in my life."

I'm one of his good things.

"I get it," I say, and honestly . . . I do. It's half, if not most, of the reason I haven't broached the subject of my feelings. There's no going back when I put my truth out there.

"I mean, I guess there's a lesson in this too, right?" Alex continues.

"What lesson is that?" I ask.

"Relationships are all bullshit. I mean, he supposedly gave up baseball for the family life, but then he gets a little attention from someone only a few years older than me, and all of a sudden his promises mean shit. Whatever. I'm too focused on baseball for all that anyhow. Who knows what kind of a cheater he would have been if he kept up with the game."

My body feels like it's sinking into the seat, as if I'm lowering through the metal and hard plastic onto the hardwood far below. I'm devastated for my friend, and even more so for his mom. And I worry how things might play out back home, how my parents will react, and a part of me also wonders about their relationship now. My dad's a pilot, and he's gone half of the time. *Does he have a Miss Arendale in some hub somewhere?*

Beyond all of these feelings fighting for attention in my brain, though, my phone has now buzzed in my back pocket twice, and I know without checking it that there are messages from Omar. I am aborting my side of the bargain, and I don't care how many cheesecakes it's going to cost me. I hope things worked out for Omar, but as much as I suck at timing, I know enough to recognize that now would be a disaster of a moment to drop a big old *I'm in love with you* on my best friend.

It's not as if I can simply leave, though. Not after all that. So instead, I'm going to have to sit here in stunned silence, my eyes darting around the court below as I pretend to be invested in this game. Our women's team is running away with it, up by twelve at the start of the fourth quarter. I would give anything for the action to pick up enough to fill these final few minutes. A close game might help Alex forget that I had something to say, too.

We sink another three.

Their superstar just fouled out.

Shit.

"Anyway," Alex says through an exhale, leaning back in a stretch. I feel his eyes on me. I'm not going to get out of this. I wonder if he saw me swallow that lump of fear just now.

"What was your thing? That's the second time I've dominated our conversation with my shit. Let's talk about you. What's going on with my best friend, huh?"

I scrunch my face then twist my mouth as I glance at Alex.

"Huh, you know what? I don't even remember what I was going to say," I lie. Poorly. And I can tell by the way he's studying me for my tells that he doesn't fully buy it. I have very obvious tells. The biggest one is rapid blinking. But I know about that one, so to combat it. I try not to blink at all. Which has become another tell, because zombie face is apparently unnerving.

"Oh, come on. I didn't mean to bring you down too. You seemed kind of hyped about whatever it is. What's up? You said you wanted to talk about something you've been feeling . . ."

My stomach drops just as Alex's eyes glance beyond my shoulder. His mouth pulls into a slight smirk, which throws me, but also gives me this weird sense of hope. He's smiling. I follow his gaze to the end of the row, where Brayden is leaning forward and looking back at us.

"Are you— Is Brayden— You want to get back with Brayden?" Alex leans back, his massive grin slapping me in the face when I jet around to face him with wide eyes.

No, no, no, no!

My mouth opens, but it's too late. Alex is already talking.

"You know he's been talking to that girl, Melissa. The one interning with the training staff," he says, the smirk still very present on his face. I hate that smirk. It's so off base. And yet, how do I tell him he's heading down the wrong path without putting him on the right one? The right one, which, of course, leads right to him—the man who just pledged himself to baseball and said relationships are for losers.

"I thought you didn't like him," he questions, brow drawn in as a surprised laugh floats past his lips.

"I don't!" And I mean it, but my words end up sounding like the rebuttal of a third grader pouting about getting out in dodgeball.

"Nik," Alex says, dropping his chin and lowering his eyes on me. His puckered smirk makes me want to cry. "Come on. It's me."

And that's the thing. Yeah, it's him. It's always him. And I was supposed to tell him that. I still could. Right now. I will. I'm going to do it.

"You know, Brayden has always been kind of jealous about you and me," he says, drawing an invisible line between our arms.

Now is the time. Do it, Nikki! Say what you feel!

"He . . . umm, he has?" I swallow hard, my mouth so dry I half expect to pull a cactus needle out from between my teeth. *Why am I so broken?*

"Oooooh, yeah. I mean, I think he just envied how close we are. Which, I get that. You and I are pretty unique."

"We are?" *Of course we are!*

"I think so." Alex shrugs. He reaches forward and takes my hand in his, weaving our fingers together, and my arm numbs from the zaps that travel up my veins.

"Just because my life's a mess doesn't mean you shouldn't be happy. If you still have a thing for our ace, I'm down to help get his attention back where it belongs." Alex taps the tip of my nose with index his finger, and I go cross-eyed watching it.

"Alex, I'm not sure—"

"*Shh*, hold on."

I hold my tongue, feeling everything and nothing at the same time. His hand is so warm, and I'm sure my palm is sweating. My pulse is beating in my fingertips. I know that much for sure.

"Yeah, he sees us," he says, turning his attention back to the game but keeping his hold on me. "Trust me, Nikki. You might not be sure, but I am." And before I can protest and put an end to this entire misunderstanding, Alex brings our tethered hands to his mouth and presses his lips to my knuckles. The whole thing lasts a second, but my eyes take it in through slow motion lenses.

"Yeah, Brayden might punch me eventually. But it will be worth it if he comes groveling back. Make him beg, though, okay? Promise me that. Make him beg for you. I think this little project is exactly what I need—a low-level distraction. I'll play fake boyfriend." Alex's eyes never fully reach mine, but his smirk shows what joy he's getting out of making his teammate jealous. Playing matchmaker. For me. With someone else.

Maybe pretend is close enough to real for me, too.

alex mendoza

I'M AN ASSHOLE.

Not only did I keep a huge secret from my best friend, but then I buried it with another one just to make myself feel better. Nikki has no idea about the beef between Brayden and me. Why would she? I barely broke the news to her about my parents; I wasn't going to pile on about how Brayden found out my dad had an affair with a former student. Just my luck that jerk is cousins with my dad's new girlfriend, Vanessa Arendale.

He's been bringing it up a little too loudly in the locker room, and last week he mentioned to some of the guys that his hot cousin works at my old school. Of course, then everyone had to stalk her social media and go on and on about how hot she is. Thank God she's savvy enough to not post photos of her with my dad being all . . . *together* and shit. Brayden's fucking face mocked me the whole time, too. I swear, the reason he's messing with me so much is because he blames me for him and Nikki breaking up—*three years ago!*

To be honest, she never seemed upset when they ended things. I'm surprised she's still into him, or whatever it is she has for him. Who am I to judge her hookups if that's what she wants. And so what if it's Brayden.

I leapt at the notion of rubbing things in his face for a little while, which wasn't doing right by Nikki. I didn't tell her this, but she could probably simply tell him she wants to start talking again and he'd be all over it. I see how he still looks at her. But selfishly? I'd rather see him work for it. I'm not sure he's good enough, but I'll put him to the test, maybe make him see what he lost when he broke up with her last time. And then when he's gotten the point, I'll let them work things out. If that's what Nikki really wants.

"Hey, in your head today, Mendoza?" Cole snaps his workout towel at my shoulder, but he's too slow, and I manage to snag it, wrap it around my fist, and jerk it from him.

"Just thinking about all the ways you suck," I joke, throwing his towel toward the trash bin. It almost goes in but slides to the floor instead.

"Ha! Yeah, good one." His wry tone prompts me to get up from the bench press and dodge his next incoming towel snap.

"Sucker, I wanted your spot," he says, taking over my bench while wearing a cocky-ass grin.

"Good luck lifting that," I say. He eyes the plates and

does the math before rolling his eyes and getting up to change them out.

Cole's an outfielder, which means he can run for miles and is probably one of two guys out here who can beat my forty time. But he can't outlift me. Only guys who can do that are Coach and our catcher, Dom.

"You psyched for Friday?" Cole asks as he ducks his head and positions himself under the bar. I move to spot him. He's still lifting too heavy. His damn ego is going to get him hurt. *Like I should talk.*

"Yeah. Hopefully I don't hit like shit," I grumble. His face muscles strain and his cheeks turn red as he lowers the weight toward his chest. I keep my hands close.

"Get out of your head. I know that's what you were in here thinking about," he huffs out once the weight is up again. He grits his teeth and begins to lower the bar again, my hands inches away.

"The draft kinda does that . . . takes over your mind?" I explain. Cole has no interest in playing beyond this year. He's already set for grad school. Dude's going to be a dentist. Maybe he has life figured out.

"You're entering a whole new era for stress," he grunts out, nodding for me to help him slide the bar back to the rack.

"That your personal best?" I ask.

"Yeah," he pants.

"Ha ha!" We slap hands and I grab hold of his to help him to his feet. "Glad my misery can give you a boost."

Cole lets out a heavy laugh as he pulls the safety clip

free from the bar to add my weight back on. I laugh along with him, but after a few seconds he's still smirking and shaking his head.

"You find my stress amusing?" I slide a weight on my end, then rest my arms on the end of the bar.

"I don't know, man. Just sayin' . . . things didn't look so stressful last night at the basketball game. I didn't know you and Nikki were finally—"

"That?" I cut him off before his gossipy mouth goes too far. "Nah, we're good friends. That's all. I was just unloading some of my stress to her is all."

I wave my hand at him then put the clip back on my side of the bar. I straddle the bench for a second and clear out my lungs with a massive exhale before positioning myself under the bar. Cole steps in to spot me, but I don't need his help for this. I've got forty more pounds to add, at least, before this lift gets hard.

"Well, you looked pretty friendly is all. And you know what? Why not? You ever think about hitting that?"

My eyes roll to meet his and I glare at him with absolute laser beams.

"Nobody *hits* Nikki," I clarify, making sure to emphasize his poor word choice with my lifted brow.

He makes the right choice and looks away as he utters, "Sorry, man. I didn't mean it like that. I get too comfortable with my words sometimes."

"Yeah, well, go ahead and forget that term. For all women. Not just Nikki." I start my lift and grunt as I push up hard and fast, meeting his eyes again. "But especially when it comes to Nikki."

I hold the weight with straight arms until he nods and says, "Understood."

I knock out eight reps in about half the time it took him, then swivel my head from under the bar so I can sit up.

"That's the thing, though. What I was saying, I mean? About you and Nikki?" I'm not following him, but if he doesn't drop my best friend from our conversation soon I might have to knock his teeth in.

"And what is the thing? Choose your words carefully," I say, pointing a finger at him as I stand and move across the room to grab my water bottle. I like getting in here about forty minutes early for weights. I like to have my space to do my work before everyone's in my way. Sure, I get in twice the workout, but also . . . *I get in twice the workout.*

"I mean, that's why it looked like maybe you two were finally getting together. It wouldn't be so crazy, you know. You're always like her big, bad bodyguard around everyone else."

I spit out half my sip of water with a hard laugh.

"Big. Bad. Bodyguard?" I don't think I'm quite that protective.

"You remember that guy from Northern State who hit on her after our series last year?" He quirks a brow, and I pretend to wrack my memory for his example. I know exactly who he means—Hunter Hyland, Northern's jackass of a relief pitcher who nailed me with a ninety-eight-mile-per-hour fastball to the ribs after spending the whole game chatting up Nikki when he should have been putting in his bullpen work.

"Come on. I know you know who I mean," Cole badgers me.

I wave him off again.

"Yeah, I know. But that was different. And so what? Nikki is important to me, and she deserves better than some guy who can only grow half a mustache." Not that I should talk about facial hair. There's a reason I stop after three days of stubble. Any more and I look like a creature from the woods.

"Look, all I'm saying is if she's that important, maybe you've been thinking about your relationship with her in the wrong way." He peers at me around the edge of his water bottle, eyebrows raised as he guzzles down a big drink.

Rather than continuing to debate him, I give him the biggest reason of all why I've never crossed that line with Nikki. There are times when it is actually the *only* reason, but it's so steadfast that it's enough.

"I hear you. And I appreciate you thinking I am even in that girl's league. But when it comes to my relationship with Nikki Thomas, it's just one of those things in life that's too important."

Cole holds my gaze for a second but eventually nods then tips his water bottle back to drain it.

Is Nikki beautiful? Yes. Is she the smartest woman I

know? Another yes. Funniest? Kindest? Most resourceful? Honest? Yeah, she's everything. It's why she's my best friend. She knows me better than anyone in my life. When I hurt, she hurts. When I fly? She flies. It's why I struggled so hard telling her the shit about my dad. But in the end, of all people, Nikki is the one I tell. And what she and I have is too important to mess up with experiments. Even if I still dream about kissing her our freshman year on a dare. We are who we are, still, because that kiss never became anything else. She was into Brayden then, and is now, apparently.

"All right, but if she wants to marry a dentist one day, you better show up to our wedding." Cole holds his serious expression in place for about half a second before a laugh breaks through half of his mouth.

"Brother, you could literally discover a new type of tooth, and there ain't no way you're getting on her radar," I jest.

Truthfully? Cole's a good looking guy. And he's nice, despite needing to work on his manners. He'd probably treat her right, too. But my blessing? Hell no. I have yet to meet the guy who gets that from me when it comes to her.

3 /
nikki

OMAR HAS OFFICIALLY CUT me off from purchasing cheesecake. Literally. I stopped in this morning at Lolo's Bake Shoppe to make good on my failure to deliver a love confession, and the worker took one look at my name on my debit card and put the slice of cheesecake I ordered away. She wouldn't let me get the cookie either. Coffee or tea, and a bagel—plain. Those were her instructions. Because those aren't things Omar likes.

He knows the sweet treats are my crutch with him. Like a get-out-of-jail free card, with excessive calories.

"Seriously? You called Lola's?" I lean on the front desk in the dorm lobby and slide him the paper bag with a single plain bagel inside.

He eyes the sack suspiciously, then unfolds the top to peek inside.

"Yeah, no. Hard pass," he says, tossing it back at me. I clutch it to my chest.

"Well, it could have been a piece of cheesecake, but *noooo!*" I bend down and tuck the bag inside my backpack, knowing I'll probably nibble at it later when I'm in my accounting class. I should have a solid business sense, but I really hate numbers that aren't associated with beats. My first indulgence if I make a go of this career will be to hire my own accountant.

"I can buy my own damn cheesecake, thank you. What I want from you is the excuse. I didn't get the full story. All you said was you'd make it up to me with cheesecake, then you slammed your door and turned up music by that girl who dances weird." He leans back in the rolling chair behind the front desk and threads his hands behind his neck as he stares me down.

"First, her name is Lorde, and she dances awesome," I say, ignoring all evidence otherwise. It's women like Lorde who pave the way to let girls like me be as strange and outside the box as we want.

"And second, he unloaded a lot of personal baggage on me before I got to say anything." I flatten my hands on the counter and tilt my head to stare right back at him. Hard.

"Really? Before you said hi he just launched right into his personal issues with you?" His smug, flat-lined mouth is annoying.

"Okay, no. I said hi when I sat down, but excuse me for not leading with 'By the way . . . I'm in love with you.'"

"*By the way* isn't necessary," Omar says, keeping his stoic expression in place. I knock over a cup of mini-pencils by my elbow, and they tumble around the computer keyboard, some falling into his lap. He gives in and laughs.

"Okay, fine. I relent. Definitely not great timing. But today—" He drops the pencils he's collected back in the cup and returns it to his desktop, just out of my reach. "Today is a new day."

His grin is obnoxious.

"Why are you so positive all the time?" I grumble, bending down to snag the strap of my backpack.

"Because *I* have a date with a lacrosse player," he brags.

I can't help the tight-lipped smile that starts to dimple my cheeks. My mission may have been a failure, but Omar had great success.

"And does this man have a name?" I quirk my brow as I sling my bag over my arms and tug it tight against my back.

"Brian. And he's pre-law. So, you know . . . we could be quite the power couple." He waggles his brows.

I point to the coffee stain in the center of his T-shirt.

"Well, you're gonna have to learn how to use a sippy first. Not a lot of power couples walking around with dribble shirt," I laugh out.

He rolls his eyes at me and grabs the napkin that he's clearly already used once this morning in an attempt to blot the stain.

"It's the damn travel cup lid. I don't get why people are so obsessed with these things." He motions to the handled cup to his right, then tucks his chin as he blots his otherwise perfect, crisp white T-shirt.

"Fair point," I say.

While he rubs the stain, which is really only making it worse, I pull my hair out of its tie and run my fingers along my scalp, straightening out the wave that always gets left behind. I pull my Chapstick from my back pocket and run it over my lips, then pull out my phone to check my face in the reverse camera.

"Yeah, not today," I say with a heavy sigh.

"You look gorgeous," my friend says. I flutter my eyes to him and purse my lips.

"I look like I haven't washed my hair in two days and got up early to hit the rec center because I wanted to avoid running into my fake boyfriend who I secretly wish was my *real* boyfriend." I shake my head and laugh at my ridiculous situation.

"Well, you're gorgeous enough for Alex to be willing to play along. So that's something," Omar reassures.

I shrug, taking the tiny win. I guess it's something that he finds me attractive enough to be into flirting. It's just that I'm not sure how to act around him. Which is simply nuts because Alex is the one person I have never felt self-conscious around. But now I am going to overthink every-thing. *Like the stupid lump in my hair from a ponytail.* I relent and put my hair back in the tie, then tell Omar to wish me luck before I take off toward the study hall room attached to the library.

Alex and I never miss a session. As an athlete, he has to log hours every week, and I've always gone with him to take advantage of the tutors and to force myself to stay on top of the homework assignments I don't love. I have an accounting project to work through today, and I'm not looking forward to it. Maybe it will distract me enough to not break down into a fit of girl giggles around my best friend.

Per usual, Alex is the only one in the room when I arrive. He's always the first to check in. It's one of his best character traits—the man is always early, and he never does anything halfway. He commits with his entire being, even to his academics. I'm not sure he's going to need his business degree once he gets drafted, but I have no doubt he'll graduate with honors. Me, however? I'll graduate with an incredibly lopsided set of transcripts. On the sound engineering side—straight As. General studies? Sometimes a C gets the job done.

Alex has his headphones on as I enter the room, his back to me. I find myself suddenly wondering how to sit with him. How do I start this interaction? What would I normally do?

How do I not remember?

I pause just inside the door and take a deep breath, letting the weight of my backpack sink into my shoulders. Shaking off the weird tingles prickling along my neck, I resolve to act as though nothing has changed at all. It's not like I told him how I feel. That . . . *that* would have made things weird. Maybe this was a blessing.

Moving in behind him, I poke his sides with my fingers, right where he's ticklish. He yelps and stands from his chair as he drops his headphones to his neck.

"Why? Every damn time!" His laugh fills the space and soothes my nerves. This is how we act. Who we are.

I shrug.

"Because I can." I toss my bag on the table and take the seat across from him.

He glares at me as he sinks back into his chair, then pulls his headphones from his neck to tuck them into his bag.

"You are the only person in the world who is not ticklish. At all. And it isn't fair." He points at me and dims his eyes. It's one of my favorite expressions he makes. I call this the playful challenge look. It's something he does for me and his mom. And I've never seen him make this face for anyone else.

"You can hit a fastball. I can withstand hours of tickle torture. I mean, it's an even trade," I say.

He chuckles and shakes his head before slinking down to get back to reading his text. He's resting his head on his fist, his eyes flickering as they scan the page, and I let myself spy on him for a few seconds before pulling out my homework. I mimic his position, the toes of our shoes touching under the table. Alex's foot has always been my doorstop. His legs are longer than mine, and without ever discussing it, we've fallen into a natural state anytime we sit across from one another where I get to rest my foot on or against his. It keeps me from sliding completely off the chair when I slump down. It's a trick I worked out in junior high in a booth at the local Denny's, and we've been doing it ever since.

We work like this in silence for about fifteen minutes before the quiet is broken by the hard laughter of the rest of the team filing into the room. Some of the football players come in here for the morning sessions too, which means it's always fairly crowded, and it doesn't take long for the other seats at our table to fill up.

"Hey, Nik. What's up?" Cole reaches a fist across the table to me and I sit up tall to tap my knuckles into his. He's my favorite of Alex's teammates. They've shared a small house together across the street from campus for the last two years. They're a good match—both more serious than others on the team. And I like that sometimes when Alex and I don't want to be the lives of a party, we can retreat to their place away from the rowdy baseball house where six of the other guys live.

Last month, Alex and I bailed on the holiday party when the drinking got a little out of hand. We fell asleep watching *A Charlie Brown Christmas* instead of spending the night throwing up in a bathroom. My head was nestled against his chest, and I let his heartbeat lull me to sleep. My gaze drifts to that spot on his chest and the tight fit of his long-sleeved white T-shirt. I've never questioned whether or not that spot on his chest is mine when I need it.

Alex's cough breaks my trance and my eyes flit up to his. He smirks.

"You spacing out there, Nik?" He drops his chin a touch, a hint of a smirk playing at his lips. I think he realizes I was staring at him. *Oh my God, was I making a swoony face?*

"I hate accounting," I retort, my answer swift.

Alex pushes his textbook toward me and spins it around.

"Wanna trade?"

My eyes scan the first line: *A study in international marketing completed by the firm of Kaufman and Stokes reveals that the concept of cryptocurrency has both advantages and risks.* I push the book back to him and make a gagging sound.

"No, thank you."

He winks as he spins his book back around. I bet he practiced that wink before he first deployed it. I think he started doing it his junior or senior year of high school. I vaguely recall some teen movie we were all into where the guy every girl was crushing over winked like that. Alex made it his own, though. It's like a token he gives out to make hearts flutter. At least, that's what it does to me. I'm good about swallowing the butterflies when they creep up, however, and hiding how happy these tiny gestures make me.

God, Nikki. At this point you might as well hang Alex's poster on your dorm room wall.

Alex is again engrossed in his boring-as-hell text. I glance up and shake my head, admonishing myself for letting the last twenty-four hours derail as badly as they have. I sit up straight and steel myself to be brave, my lips parting and the words *I'm really not into Brayden* about to fall from my mouth when the only person, perhaps on the planet, who can make my insides boil with jealous rage saunters behind Alex.

Alicia's gaze hits me briefly as she brushes her fingertips along Alex's shoulder and the back of his neck. He startles, his head jerking around. I bet he was expecting to find one of his teammates fucking with him, but instead, he got his former . . . whatever he and Alicia were. He relaxes back into his seat and twists to open his stance to her. She's standing closer than any normal acquaintance would, hovering on the verge of being between his knees as he looks up at her. Alicia's glossy red lips flash that superior smirk. That look, it's for me.

"Hi, Alicia," I say, leaning forward and resting both elbows on the table as I prop my chin on my fists. I give her a different kind of grin, the kind that says *you're a bitch.*

"Nicole," she drones, using my formal name, which not even my mother uses.

"*Hmm,*" I say with a slight nod, acknowledging the ice between us. I've never liked Alicia. I don't trust her. I'm certain that sentiment is mutual. It's not the kind of thing she and I need to hash out so we can be friends. We're too different. And I don't want to be her friend. I want to graduate and never see her face again. Three years of maturity and growth does wonders for the backbone. At least it did for me when it comes to dealing with girls like Alicia.

Alex, however, only cuts people out of his life if they've

cheated on his mom. And since he and Alicia have history, he's always kind to her. Which is noble of him, and makes him . . . *him*. All my jaded self sees is the girl who manipulated me into kissing my best friend for the first time in front of her, simply so she could diminish it. And I'd bet my life on the fact she has a similarly unflattering opinion of me.

"You coming to the game Friday? Opening day." Alex glances at me, that twinkle in his eyes. He's still a kid when it comes to his excitement for baseball.

"Yeah. I'd love to," Alicia basically squeals. The study room monitor hushes her.

"Great. *See ya then*," Alex says, sending her off with a nod. And then . . . a wink. *Dammit. He gave her one too.*

The muscles around my mouth twitch, and I know I'm doing a poor job of hiding my reaction. The pursing of my lips deepens at the corners, and I can't get it in check before Alex glances back to me.

"Oh, stop. You never liked her. If she shows up Friday, be nice."

I shake with a short, silent laugh. It's not like I'm going to start a brawl or anything. Now, imagine one? Sure. I'll imagine clawing her eyes out all day. But, acting on those impulses? No, even I know it wouldn't be my best look. And it would be from a really bitter place. But I don't have to worry about any of that.

"She's not showing up for your game," I toss out, rolling my eyes and forcing myself to focus on my homework.

"She might," he says in an offhanded way. I know he's not really trying to defend her, but rather trying to soften me. I'm irritable, though, so I react, snorting another quick laugh.

"What's that for?"

I close my eyes for a second and exhale through my nose. I hate when he calls me out for being snarky. But also, I'm not wrong. And maybe if I told him how I felt yesterday, or the day before, or any day we've been together, then I wouldn't be lugging around the jealousy beast all the time. The one that refuses to give Alicia any credit for supporting Alex's dreams.

I open my eyes and meet his gaze.

"Because when you dated, she never showed up for a game. Not once." I shrug as Alex stares on, squinting slightly in suspicion.

"Nah, she came to a few."

I shake my head, and a suffocating weight crushes my chest. Alex's expression is caught between serious and playful, the faint curve to his lips softening as his eyes try to read me.

"How do you know?" he finally asks.

My lips twist, a strange invisible force pressing me on all sides. For a beat, I consider shrugging it off and saying maybe I'm wrong. But I'm not wrong. And more than that, it hurts a little that he doesn't know why I'm so certain. I've never missed one.

"Because I would have seen her there."

His eyes flinch slightly. It's enough to spark a shift in

his overall expression, the playful look in his eyes morphing to reflect enlightenment, maybe. Doubt, perhaps.

Or—what has my stomach in knots—the realization that I have always shown up. For him. And maybe there's a deeper reason why.

I HAVEN'T BEEN RIGHT in the head since summer. Since I found out about my parents' split and my dad's . . . extra-curricular activities. I've felt so many things— embarrassed, angry, betrayed. Mostly, though, I've felt alone.

That's my fault. I don't know why I didn't tell Nikki. No, that's a lie. I know. Shame is the easy answer, but the truth is my parents were once best friends, too. And look how my dad fucked that all up. I can't lose Nikki. It's why I drew the line at friends in high school. And damn, that wasn't easy, because when Nikki decided to start wearing crop tops and tight jeans all the time, I had to put away the sweat pants and stick to jeans. The last thing I needed was for her to catch me popping a boner when I drove her to school in the morning.

I may have been a hormone-fueled dumbass at sixteen, but I had enough smarts to know that Nikki Thomas was more to me than just some really great curves. And I mean *great* curves. That have only gotten so much greater. *So, so much greater.* But it's the other things she is—my steady, my conscience, my roots—that has always kept me in check.

And if I start to forget that, I'm sure one call from my mom will remind me.

My mom has been calling daily. This afternoon, it was to gripe about how mushy Wela's carne asada was, and how she's worried her mom is starting to forget things because she spaced and let it marinate for almost eighteen hours. Last week, we talked about the to-do list of things my mom needed done around the house, stuff I'm sure my dad would gladly do, but my mom is too proud to ask. I don't blame her. Two best friends in the coldest of wars. They can't even call each other.

I can't imagine not being able to call Nikki. To tell her about my day. About how fucking stressed I am that I'm going to blow it my senior year and not make the draft. Or about how much it sucks to watch my family fall apart. I kept my parents' split from her for months, and it was torture. To lose that connection—my person—forever . . . well, it's simply not worth the risk.

What we are now is too important.

"Dude, your heart isn't even in this," Cole says, tossing his controller onto the coffee table after kicking my ass in *Super Smash Bros.* for a fifth time.

"Sorry. I really wanna go hit, but I know I can't hit twenty hours a day to get out of my slump. I have to—"

"Trust the process," we both say in unison, laughing. My laugh, though, is shorter.

I've been trying for weeks now to trust that my hard work will pay off. No, for months. My fall numbers were shit. And Edwin's were good. I'm not sure how long that faith Coach seems to have in me is going to hold up over common sense. We need to win games, and if Edwin's bat in the lineup does that more than mine, well . . .

"Hey, did you know Nikki hasn't missed a single game?" My brain hasn't been able to lose this detail since she said it. I keep ruminating on it.

Cole laughs hard from the kitchen. He comes out with two beers, handing me one then flopping back down into the well-worn sofa cushion before rolling his head to the side and hitting me with the *duh* look.

"No, like, I mean even the away ones," I explain.

Cole blinks slowly then holds out his palm as if to say —*duh*. Again.

I *tsk* and shake my head, not wanting to go down this road with him. Yeah, Nikki and I are good together. Like friends. We're friends.

"Are you telling me you never thought about that?"

I nod and reach for my controller, wishing I hadn't started this. "Yeah, yeah. It was just on my mind, is all."

Cole grabs his controller and pauses the game I just started. I press begin again and he pauses right away.

"Fuck, man. Alright! She goes to all my games. I'm oblivious. What do you want?" I toss the controller again.

At this point I'd rather punch my friend for real rather than on the video game.

He chuckles.

"She borrows your car to drive to the away games. Some of those are far. And yeah, usually she can drag a friend along to split a hotel room, or she makes the drive back and forth every night because she has to be in the dorm for her job. But sometimes, she drops the money to stay on her own and sticks around by herself. You, my friend, are an idiot."

His laugh is different this time. Frustrated. Fuck, maybe I'm frustrated with me too.

"Yeah, well, I don't ask her to do that." I squeeze my eyes shut as soon as the words come out because what a dick thing to say. And I don't mean it.

Cole gets up and shakes his head, looking down at me.

"You don't get it, man. You don't *have* to ask her." He leaves me with what I already know and goes to his room, shutting the door.

Great. More time by myself with my thoughts.

I grab the TV remote, flip the setting to put the Cubs game on and turn the volume down to a low mumble. It makes me feel less alone.

My phone buzzes in my pocket so I shift and pull it out to see a text from Nikki, and all I can do is laugh to myself. Of course she's texting now, when my head's a mess with thoughts of her. I'm sure if Cole were still out here he'd bust a gut at the irony. Or he'd call it fate or some annoying shit that probably has some truth to it.

NIKKI: Hey, I need help getting my numbers to line up. Do you have a sec?

I breathe out and weigh the time, 10:14, against my instincts. I could say I'm almost asleep. It's a practice night so not weird that I'd knock off early. But then she'd spend the next however many hours on YouTube trying to figure out what she's doing wrong in the accounting software.

I hit the call icon and bring my phone to my ear.

"Oh, thank God," she answers.

I chuckle.

"That bad, huh?" I carry my beer into the kitchen and drop it in the sink. I barely took a sip and if this is as rough as I expect it is, I'm going to need to head over there.

"Alex, I don't even know how I did this, but I somehow copied everything twice, and now it looks like my fake company is embezzling money or . . . I don't know, printing their own! Can you help?"

I smirk at her exasperated tone. I can picture her pacing, hands gesticulating as she points and blames the computer. She's a wiz on that soundboard. I don't know how none of that translates to other technology.

"Okay, hit pause and do not touch anything else. I'll be there in two."

"Thank you. And I won't even talk near my computer. I swear it's listening and doing things to screw with me." She hangs up and I stare at the ended call screen, amused.

I glance at Cole's shut door and chew at my mouth for

a few seconds. I'm glad he left and isn't here to see this. I'm sure he'd have a full evaluation of how I'm about to go running over when Nikki calls. But that's nothing new. Which again, he'd probably point that out too.

I lock up, jump in the car, and make it to the visitor lot for Nikki's dorm in minutes. She has her door propped open when I arrive, so I close it behind me. She's sitting cross-legged in the middle of her bed, rubbing her temples and staring at her screen.

"Are you trying to mentally bend it to your will?"

She blinks up with wide eyes and gritted teeth.

"Oh, I'm willing things at it. Like, to catch on fire." She nudges her laptop so the screen faces me.

"I wouldn't recommend that. This building is pretty old and it would go up like that," I say with a finger snap before taking her computer and sitting at the end of her bed with my back against the wall. I prop the computer on my lap and gesture with my head for her to scoot next to me.

"Come learn," I say.

"Ugh, do I have to? Can't you just . . . I don't know. Do it?" She flits her fingers at her computer as if sprinkling magic at it, and I laugh out once.

"You know my stance on cheating," I lob back at her. She rolls her eyes and utters, "Cheaters never win," in the whiniest voice she can muster. Funny how that mantra I have thrown at her our whole lives every time she tries to cheat at Uno or board games has a whole different connotation now. There's a different kind of cheater in my life.

The short silence left in the void indicates Nikki might realize this new double-meaning too. After a few quiet seconds, she drags her body over to me, her face sour. Flopping on her stomach, she shoves a pillow under her chest and arms to help support her upper body as she lies next to me and peers at the computer screen.

"This isn't going to be as hard as you think," I begin, clicking open a window at the top right of the screen. Nikki's head bops up and she taps on where I clicked.

"Wait a second, there's stuff in there? Like . . . how would I ever know to click on that?" she gripes.

I peer down at her, my mouth a sarcastic tight line.

"I suspect that this was probably covered in one of those slideshows you slept through."

Her gaze shifts to me, her expression matching mine, though her tight-lined mouth due less to sarcasm and more to aggravation.

"Maybe I'm tired because I have to drive all over the Midwest going to baseball games," she says, her eyes blinking rapidly the moment the words escape her.

"Wow." My brow flirts with my hairline as I hold her gaze. She clears her throat and looks at the screen again.

"Sorry, I didn't mean it like that," she says. Her eyes flit to me once more, briefly. "Really. I'm sorry."

I don't know how to respond, so I shift my body to get more comfortable and to turn the screen more in her direction while I click around a few options and clear the duplicate entries in her account.

"And that should always show zero when it's right," I say, hovering the cursor over the two total sums.

She slaps her hands to her cheeks, dragging the bottoms of her eyes down as her mouth hangs open.

"You fixed it in like four minutes."

"More like ten, but . . . yeah." I click save and move the computer to her bed.

I lie down and prop my head on an elbow as she sits and takes over to turn in her assignment remotely. The light music in the background is a familiar mix. It's one she made freshman year, all R&B blending old and new. It's smooth.

"I always liked this one," I say, leaning my head toward the Bose speaker on her dresser.

She snaps her laptop shut and runs her palms over the surface, seemingly relieved to have that assignment done. She grins at me, always proud of her work. She should be.

"Yeah? I should send you the link. This one's good for stress." She leans to the side to set her laptop on the night table, trading it out for her phone. A few seconds later I feel mine buzz in my pocket.

"There. Sent."

"Thanks," I say, smiling on one side of my mouth.

She sees right through me. I bet Nikki sensed there was more to my stress long before I told her about my parents. She's always so tuned in, usually more than I am to myself. I should try harder to give her the same kind of support. Maybe I'm a shitty friend.

"I'm sorry I didn't tell you right away," I say, my racing

thoughts finding their way out of my mouth. She tosses her phone on the bed and shifts to lie opposite me, propping her head up the same.

"*Hmm?* Oh, about your parents? I understand—"

"Seriously, Nik," I interrupt, circling her wrist with my other hand. She takes in a sharp breath, so I run my thumb along her skin. I meant that to be tender.

"Sorry, I didn't mean to scare you. I just want you to know that I appreciate how you're always there for me. And I'm sorry I didn't trust that."

Her gaze locks on mine and her nostrils flex with a breath.

"*Mmm hmm,*" she says with a tiny nod.

I squeeze her wrist and let go, instantly calculating how thin her wrist feels in my grip, how smooth her skin is, how hard her pulse beats, and how still she is. Nikki plays tough, but she's also breakable. I have to protect her.

"It means a lot to me," I say, and her eyes draw in, her brow puzzling.

"Alex, were you afraid I'd judge you? Because of your dad? It's me. It's . . . us."

I flatten my arm on her mattress and lower my head to my bicep as I shrug.

"Not really. But if I'm being honest . . . I'm pretty embarrassed by him." Mortified, really. Odell is a small town, and what he did won't be a secret for much longer, no matter how hard my mom tries to keep it one. And then people will talk, and going home won't feel like *going home* anymore.

"I understand. But he's not you." Nikki reaches for me this time, her palm curving over my shoulder. For the first time, maybe ever, I'm singularly focused on the way her hand feels on my skin. Her palm is cool, but not cold. The hard edge of her thumbnail tickles along my shoulder. It's somehow sharp yet soft. Her focus is on her touch, but mine is on her eyes. I've always known they're this strange mix of green and brown, but I've never really appreciated how unique they are. Suddenly, her gaze shifts, and she catches me. Her hand freezes, then balls into a fist that she tucks against her chest as it slips away from my arm .

"Thank you for coming to my games. All of them, I mean. I should say that more." I should tell her she doesn't have to and relieve her of the pressure, but I want her there. When my game is off, knowing she's there rooting for me somehow makes me fight through the doubt.

"I wouldn't miss them for the world," she says.

We lie in quiet for several seconds, eyes locked. It's strange how it's both easy and uncomfortable at the same time.

"I should go," I finally let out.

"You can stay. If . . . if you're tired, I mean. Just get up early." Her shoulder quirks up a tick along with one side of her mouth. I've slept in the same bed with her, this bed even, so many times—watching a movie, studying for finals, listening while she works on a mix—but this tightness in my chest feels like a warning. If I stay here, those thoughts might get messy, and I might do something stupid.

"I should go," I repeat, giving her a soft smile as I sit up and lean toward her to kiss the side of her head. My lips tingle despite having kissed her like that—exactly like that—a week ago.

Her lopsided smile is locked in place as I stand, but her eyes aren't smiling. She knows I need to leave. To protect us.

I make my way to her door and crack it open before pausing and looking back. She's still lying in the same position, expression frozen in time.

"Hey, live batting practice tomorrow. Brayden's throwing a session. Maybe to me, who knows. You coming? You can cheer for both of us, I mean. Me a little louder, of course."

Her mouth curves a tiny bit more.

"I wouldn't miss it for the world."

She blinks slowly, and for a flash of a second I play out a world where I drop the door shut again and rush to the bed, caging her under my body and between my arms. I clear it away immediately. I open the door wider instead, and glance at her over my shoulder as I leave.

"Good night, Nik."

5 /
nikki

I DIDN'T SLEEP at all, basically. And since I turned in my accounting assignment on time, I feel that warrants me skipping today's lecture and taking it easy until Alex has batting practice. My professor posts his lectures in our group chat anyhow, so I can catch up later. Or maybe have Alex show me how to do whatever the project is. Of course, that's what led to me not sleeping in the first place, so I'm not so sure that's a sustainable plan.

I don't think I care, though. Because last night, there was something there between us that I haven't felt since we were forced to kiss our freshman year. There was this tug, and I know I didn't imagine it. I'm sure it's the reason Alex left so fast. Usually he sticks around and watches viral videos with me or plows through whatever leftovers I have stashed away in my fridge.

Damn, do I wish I wasn't a chickenshit and had the guts to go for it with him. To say it once out loud. To just ask him to kiss me, one more time, for real. Just to see.

I wonder what he would have done if I just went ahead and kissed him. We were close enough.

Of course, what would happen if he stopped me and told me I was making a mistake? That . . . that would destroy me. I'd lose hope, sure, but also . . . I'd lose Alex.

"Gah!" I groan, pushing my headphones from my ears and rolling to my back. I reach to the side and push my laptop shut. I've been working on this new mix since about three in the morning, and I'm not sure what's wrong with it. No matter how much I mess with the midrange, it still sounds off. Everything I try sounds the same, and it's stuck in this flat place where nothing stands out. I need this sound to more than stand out; I need it to bully its way into the ears of every sound manager I send it to so I can land an apprenticeship in the next six months.

The familiar slow knock on my door is a good excuse to put the headphones away. I begged Omar to come with me to watch Alex hit today. I think the only reason he agreed is because the lacrosse field is right next to the baseball stadium.

"Come in," I say, bending down with my head between my legs so I can scan the floor under my bed for my sneakers. There's a chill in the air today, despite the sun. It sucks that baseball season in the Midwest starts under the constant threat of snow, but the cold has never bothered Alex. He says he prefers to play in it, but I don't know—I see the pictures of spring ball in Arizona and Florida and it looks pretty nice.

"You trying a new stretch out or something?" Omar says just as I spot my right sneaker hidden behind a sweatshirt under my bed.

"Navigating my mess," I say, bringing my head up and flinging my hair back. The room swirls for a few seconds and I pinch the bridge of my nose.

"You planning on navigating *that* mess?" Omar motions to my head and I pat my hands on either side to see if he's just teasing me. My fingers get snarled in tangles.

"Well, shit," I grumble, slipping my shoes on then moving to my vanity to force my hairbrush through some serious bedhead.

"I'm assuming that isn't sex hair?" he teases.

I give him a middle finger with my free hand while brushing with the other.

I work out most of the snarls and compromise with my favorite dark blue beanie. I snag the matching sweatshirt from the floor and shove my phone and keys into my pockets before holding my arms out for Omar to give me a quick once over.

"Hot," he says, and I'm not sure whether he's teasing or being sincere. I scowl at him as I pass, deciding he's likely ribbing me.

"Hey, I'm sure that look *is* hot to some people," he laughs out.

I keep walking, satisfied enough that if this look is hot to anyone, it would be Alex. I've caught him checking out my ass before in these jeans. And maybe he's been up all night thinking, too. I hold on to the positive thought that anything—meaning a world where Alex admits to always loving me as well—is possible. That bubble stays intact all the way to the stadium. Until I see Alicia sitting in the very spot I like to sit. Always. For every game.

I make a dead stop on the small concourse on the third base side, and Omar catches on a few steps ahead of me. He follows my gaze to my nemesis, who he is well versed in thanks to many late nights of box wine and cheesecake.

"Please don't get in a fight. I know I look strong, but I really don't want to get punched." His head swivels as he glances back to Alicia's profile then again to me.

"I don't think the five-two girl is picking a fight with the six-two mass of male muscle, but I'll keep it in check." My eyes flutter closed before I get a chance to roll them with my sarcasm.

"You did say he invited her," Omar reminds me.

"Yeah, to the game! Not practice. And I swore she wouldn't come. And here we are. Thanks for getting me caught up on the facts." I pinch the bridge of my nose and look down at my feet as I let out a heavy sigh and hold up my hand.

"I'm sorry. That was bitchy."

"It was. But I forgive you. Come on. Let's pick some new favorite seats." Omar loops his arm in mine and we travel to the opposite side, which means I'll be watching Alex hit from behind.

My base instincts never mind this vantage point, but the best friend part of my core prefers to be able to watch his mechanics. I'm sure he wants me to record his swings. My cloud storage basically houses his future documentary tape, given how much gameplay and other Alex practice video I have saved. He likes to look at his swing and break it down, find areas for improvement, or hints at what could be going wrong. To me, that part always feels like self-abuse, watching a failure over and over again. But it's what Alex's dad taught him, and despite the rift in their relationship, it's a practice he adheres to. I was filming batting practice in the tunnels for him last week.

Omar and I slip into a pair of seats about ten rows up behind the dugout. I take the aisle so I can run down and sit closer to video when Alex is up. Unfortunately, this spot also means I'm practically staring at Alicia while she taps away at her phone, her feet crossed on the armrest of the seat in front of hers. She shouldn't get credit for being here.

"Stop it," Omar says, nudging my knee with his.

"I can't."

"I know. But try."

He's right. I nod my head and retrain my focus to the field. Cole was hitting when we walked up which means Alex's group should be next. Brayden must have pitched to the first group because his arm is wrapped with ice. I'm sure they're playing it safe with him to keep his arm healthy for opening day. I catch his eye as he leans forward to spit out some seeds, and he awkwardly lifts his wrapped arm to say hi. I laugh softly and hold up an open palm in return.

"Are we flirting with the enemy?" Omar jests.

"God, no. Just being nice." I drop my hand to rest on my thigh and redirect my focus to the familiar shortstop taking practice swings behind home plate.

When Alex pauses, I scoot to the edge of my seat and sit up tall in an effort to get his attention. He squints against the harsh afternoon sun that reflects off of the puffy clouds. It's strange how it can be so sunny yet so freezing cold. He's scanning my usual section, and thankfully Alicia is still typing away on her phone and misses him spotting her. I'm not sure my mouth is strong enough to remain shut if she does that bunchy hand wave thing to him right now. Alex continues to scan the seats, which are mostly empty except for a few clusters of parents, a student reporter, and some diehard local fans. He nods when our eyes finally meet, and I hold up my phone. He gives me a thumbs up then holds up two fingers, I think letting me know he'll hit second in his group.

"I'm going to scoot down close to video. I'll be right back," I say to Omar, who waves me on. His attention has drifted to the lacrosse field, where practice seems to be wrapping up.

I plant myself right above the dugout, just out of the coach's view. Resting my elbows on the concrete surface, I frame my shot while the first batter takes his swings. The hitting turtle backstop limits my angle, but I manage to find the right spot to get a clear shot of Alex's footwork. Too bad he can't switch hit and take a few swings from the right for me. I've never understood how he could throw with one hand but hit from the opposite side only. It's another habit influenced by his father's coaching, and now it's set in stone.

I check my focus one last time, change around a few settings, and notice movement in the background. I keep that part blurry on camera, but when I look up, I manage to catch Brayden talking to another pitcher outside the other dugout. He seems to be showing him a grip technique. It's rare to see him give advice to anyone unless it's how to properly admire him. I snicker to myself at that thought.

When it's finally Alex's turn, I start recording early to make sure I get the focus right before he starts taking swings. I'm so focused on him that I don't realize they've switched pitchers too. But the second Alex takes his first hack, swinging for the fences on a slider that runs away from him, I become keenly interested in who could have thrown something by him.

It's the guy Brayden was giving tips to, and it seems he's got some good stuff. All well and good for him, I'm sure, as he's probably trying to work into a solid spot in the bullpen. But for a slugger who's trying to pull himself out of a slump, having a pitcher show off is not great timing.

"Come on, Alex. Dig deep," I mutter, not even caring that he'll hear it when he watches this back later.

I study him through my phone screen, opting to watch his swings through the filter of my phone rather than in real life right in front of me. I'm afraid I'll shift and not get him in frame because I tend to twist my torso along with him when he hits. Pitch after pitch, I find I'm twisting less as Alex takes one rough swing after another. He fouls about six pitches into the third base dugout, one whizzing by Brayden's head. He manages to work a full count, but ultimately, the hotshot on the mound dishes him the same pitch he started with, and Alex's legs crumple as he swings at a ball that trails at least four balls outside.

"Dammit," I utter after stopping the recording.

Alex's nostrils flare as he rounds the backstop. His gaze passes over me, our eyes locking for the briefest moment, just long enough for me to catch the glossiness. He's letting his frustration take over everything, and I haven't seen this happen to him since we were teenagers and he was fighting for an all-star bid in the playoffs.

I get up from my crouching position and slide back into the seat, glancing over my shoulder to Omar. He lifts a shoulder in a shrug and winces. Even he knows that wasn't Alex's typical stuff.

I hold up a finger and mouth *one more round*. Omar points with his thumb over his shoulder toward the lacrosse field, where the players are packing up. I wave him on, and his ridiculously wide grin as he practically jets from his seat and rushes up the stadium steps makes me so happy for him. As long as we've been friends, I've never known Omar to be smitten with someone. He's usually jaded about relationships, having had some pretty bad false starts.

Indulging in a quick glance to Alicia, I unfortunately

make eye contact with her. She holds up a hand, but it's obvious in her stilted movement that it's more of an acknowledgement rather than an actual hello or *good to see you*. I mimic the move and hold my mouth in a tight-lipped smile, hoping to convey *fuck off*.

She leans forward and turns her attention to Alex as if she's been watching him the whole time. I'd love to snoop her social media posts to see what she was really doing for the last twenty minutes but I don't want to clear the video settings on my phone.

Alex is standing closer to me than before but I don't dare talk to him. He needs to stay focused, and Coach doesn't like distracted players. I scootch over a seat so I'm shielded more by the dugout and turn my focus to Edwin, the star freshman who is now taking swings against the same pitcher. He gets a first pitch fastball that he sends to the fence, and I wince and sit up tall to take a peek at Alex's reaction. He's stopped his practice swings and is simply watching. My heart aches because I know he's sick seeing this.

Edwin fouls off a few off-speed pitches then swings and misses on another fastball, but Coach tells him to take one more before he leaves the batter's box. The pitcher may as well have served it on a platter because Edwin digs in with a full leg kick and knocks the ball off the left field foul pole, the reverberation like someone rang a bell to alert the village. I'm sure Alex is thinking they're announcing the arrival of the new king. He's going to let this get into his psyche. I know it.

Alex is up next, and the hotshot pitcher hit his count for the day, so he gets to hit off of a pitcher he's more familiar with. I hope it helps him find some confidence, but I know how Alex thinks—he wants to prove himself against the other guy. Against Edwin.

After a few warm-up throws, Alex steps in and I set up to film. The first pitch comes in right down the pipe and Alex drills it down the first base line. He rolls his shoulders after the swing and digs his back foot in more. He's anxious, which is obvious in the way he leaps on the next two pitches and sends them foul, one crawling up the third-base wall and into the seats. One of the kids out here watching practice sprints to collect the souvenir.

Alex backs out for a second, holding up a hand to take time. Coach is leaning against the side of the dugout with his arms crossed, his sunglasses doing little to mask the fact he's staring right at his star player. Probably wondering if he can be fixed. Alex takes a deep breath and blows it out hard, dropping the tension from his shoulders before rolling them one last time. He sets up in the box and nods that he's ready.

"You got this," I hum.

The pitch sails in at what feels like mid-nineties, maybe a hundred. It's dead center. And Alex doesn't even flinch.

"Strike three!"

The pitching coach is calling balls and strikes, and he's a little pumped that one of his guys got the punch-out. Alex is less enthused, though, and tosses his bat toward the dugout as he pulls his helmet off and shouts, "Fuck!" on his way in. Coach's head swivels as he passes. He's clearly giving Alex the stare-down. There's a fine line between loving a player's passion and thinking they need an attitude adjustment.

Shit.

I move back to my original seat and tuck my phone into my back pocket. Alicia has gotten to her feet and pulled on the ridiculously furry coat she brought out with her. It's cold but it's not snowing, for Pete's sake. She's hovering in the aisle, and every time Alex paces from the water cooler back to the dugout she pops up on her toes and holds up a hand to get his attention. She's trying to leave but get credit. I know it in my gut, and I can't help but feel amused that she's so clueless about what Alex needs right now.

He finally seems to acknowledge her, giving her a nod, and she gathers up her massive purse and pulls her jacket tight as she heads through the main gates. I shouldn't feel so smug given that my friend is having a dream crisis in front of me, but I'm so glad she's gone.

The rest of the hitting groups finish up over the next thirty minutes, and Alex volunteers to shag balls, going extra hard to spoil what would be good hits if he weren't out there fielding them. Some of the guys call him out for it, but he doesn't stop, even diving a few times to make a stop at short. My chest hurts for him, because I know what he's doing. He's trying to show his worth, to Coach, and to himself. He may have sucked hitting today, but he wants the world to know he can still field better than any player on this roster. And I'm guessing it's because he can that Coach lets him work out his shit on the field without telling him to stop.

Practice ends and the players clear out, a few lingering behind to put the batting turtle away and rake the field. Brayden takes the long route around, and I know it's so he can stop by and talk to me. I tense up as he gets closer, catching Alex's gaze from across the field as he drags a rake around third base. He stops and leans his weight on it as Brayden steps through the gate, and I get a tightness in my chest, like I'm somehow betraying Alex by talking to him.

"You missed me. I threw first and I put on a show," Brayden says, stopping a row in front of me and popping a foot up on a seat so he can rest his crossed forearms over his thigh. I smirk a little because having dated him freshman year I recognize the various ways he likes to peacock. This pose flexes his leg muscles and shows off his forearms. I'm not so jaded that I can't admit they're mighty nice to see.

"Yeah? You pitch to the other pitchers?" I joke, knowing pitchers don't hit and implying that he struck out the worst bats on the team.

His head rears back and he coughs out what sounds like a genuine laugh.

"No, but I've had bad days when even those guys could rake off of me." His blue eyes crinkle at the sides with his smile. He's a pretty man. Always has been. He just knows it.

"You coming to the house party Saturday night?" he asks.

I glance to Alex, who is still watching the two of us from out on the field. Brayden follows my gaze and nods.

"Ah, gotta ask your boy. You two . . . finally . . ." He swirls his finger in the air as his gaze shifts back to me.

"No, we're . . . I don't know," I stammer, suddenly more confused than ever.

My pulse races with panic, and fight or flight takes over. I stand and shove my hands in my back pockets, the ends of my hair not tucked in my hat whipping across my face as the wind picks up.

"Well, I'm inviting you," he says, pulling his hat from his head and running his forearm across his brow. There's no sweat there. He did that for effect. God, I know all of his moves.

"Thanks. Yeah, I'll . . . try to make it," I say, shuffling my way down the row and away from him.

I glance at Alex again, and he starts to move the rake around. Brayden chuckles.

"Alright, then. I hope you do. I'd love to catch up, see how the music is going," he says, and the fact he drops that little line hooks my chest and tugs. I don't let it show in my steps or my expression, instead smiling and waving bye, but the fact he made the effort to note something that is mine means something. In the months we dated he never took an interest, not once. Alex flirts with me a few times and suddenly Brayden wants to be present. I really don't want him to be, but it's also kind of nice.

I squeeze my eyes shut when I get to the side gate and flop my back against the wall outside the door to the club-house. I push my fists in my eyes and groan quietly. How did I get into this situation? And what was that little alpha display Alex put on with the death stare?

I nod to a few of the guys as they walk out after changing, keep my head down, and pretend to be reading my phone when the coaching staff passes. Alex has a key since he's a senior leader, so I'm sure he'll be locking up. After about ten minutes, everyone else is gone, and Alex ambles through the gate, stopping the minute his cleats hit the concrete. The weight of the world—his world—is pulling down his shoulders, his eyes, his mouth, his very being. He drops his gear bag at his feet and shrugs.

Now isn't the time for me to sort through my mess. My friend needs me. I give him a soft smile and step into him, letting him wrap his arms around me and sink his face into the side of my neck. His arms are heavy on my shoulders and his chest shakes. I rub my palms in circles around his back, then clutch him against me tightly as he lets it out, my neck damp with his tears.

"I'm fucking blowing it," he mumbles against my skin.

"You're not, Alex. I promise you. You're not." Even though I'm not sure that's true, it's what he needs to hear. And it's the only way he can pull himself out of this. He needs me, his best friend. And that's what I'll be.

6 /
alex

I WANTED TO WALLOW, but Nikki insisted I follow the routine. Wednesday night fish fry at Patty's is a meal never to be missed. It doesn't hurt that it's all you can eat for nine-ninety-nine. Plus, it's baseball tradition. The guys always go. And if I start to pull away from the team, I'm only going to make myself look more pathetic. Like I don't have this under control.

But I don't. And I can't seem to find my way back.

Today was a whole new level of being in my own head. It's as if Chase, the young arm we recruited over break, knew all my weaknesses. I couldn't get a handle on his routine. It didn't help that I was the first guy he faced, but then when I watched him pitch to the other guys—to Edwin—it was like they got something entirely different.

I shake my head and remind myself of Nikki's words. For now, we focus on dinner, darts, and dancing. I can go back to obsessing in the morning. I promised her I'd do my best.

Nikki sets a pitcher on the table and I push her basket of fish and chips toward her. Cole slips into one of our open seats.

"Got room for this meathead?" He gestures over his shoulder to Cutter McCreary. I smirk and stand to give him a bro hug. Cutter and I went through Tiff freshman orientation together. He's a good guy, even though he's a hockey player. The hockey team at this school gets treated like royalty. Pisses a lot of us other athletes off.

"Man, what's up? Last time I saw you, *hmm*"—I hold my finger to my chin, playing it up—"I think Laney Price hated your ass." I poke at his ribs and the fucker actually blushes.

"Yeah, well. I bet if you asked her, there are still days she hates me," he laughs out. I chuckle with him.

His girlfriend might be the best athlete this school has ever seen, and she's fierce in general. When the hockey team took over the women's locker space, Laney led the battle to make sure the hockey program, and mostly its captain, Cutter, suffered. How the hell the two of them ended up being campus *it* couple after all that baffles me.

Cutter pushes around me, effectively knocking me onto my ass on my stool, so he can give Nikki a proper hug. She slides off her stool and licks the fish fry grease from her fingertips then leaps at him, casting her arms around his neck as he lifts her up and swings her around. It's nothing new for them—they've been friends since orientation too—but for some reason, the sight of his hands on her shoulder blades has me running hot.

"Where is Laney?" I blurt out. I force an overly large smile on my face, but Cole coughs out a laugh because nothing gets by him.

"She's getting extra reps. Her draft is soon," Cutter says, dropping Nikki back down to earth as if he's a Hemsworth brother. He pulls a free stool over to our table and holds up a hand, which immediately ushers a server to our table with a pitcher in hand.

Fucking hockey dudes, man.

I pour my beer then tip back my mug, guzzling down a third of it to wash away this weird jealous wave smacking into my chest. Gazing over the rim of my glass, I lock eyes with Brayden, who is staring hard at our table, clearly nursing a jealous wave of his own. Shit, I'm no better than he is.

Without thinking, I hook my foot around the leg of Nikki's stool and scoot her close enough for me to put my hand on her knee. She coughs out a *whoa* from the not-so-gentle motion.

"You got something," I say, running the side of my finger along her cheek. Her eyes dim and then flit toward Cole. There's nothing on her face, but Brayden sure didn't like watching me touch her.

"Got it," I say, giving her a quick smile. Her brow furrows, so I nod over her shoulder. She twists her head, her hair dragging along her shoulders as she glances at where Brayden sits with some of the other pitchers, including the guy who wiped the floor with me today.

"Ah," she says, swiveling back to face me. Her hair gets

caught in the collar of her sweatshirt, so I slip my hand around her neck and pull it free. I leave my hand on her skin, my thumb grazing the top of her spine. Her skin is so hot. And soft.

Cole coughs, and I shake my head and pull my hand away.

"Sorry, you were going to hang yourself with that head of hair," I say.

She gives me a sideways look and mutters out, "Okay," before pulling her beanie from her back pocket and tugging it down on the top of her head. I smirk at her attempt to hide herself. She's always done that, but I don't think it has the same effect she thinks it does.

Nik has always been able to pull off hats. Ballcaps, cowboy hats, those giant sun-stoppers the old ladies wear near our hometown senior center. Hell, she even looks good in visors. But beanies are definitely her vibe. She has this tough chick thing going, which I know carries plenty of legitimacy.

The table is quiet for about five minutes while we all devour the greasiest food this side of the Mississippi. I'm not even certain there's actual fish in these things. I'm not sure it matters with the amount of batter, salt and Patty's special seasoning. It's a good thing this is only on the menu once a week.

"What do you say, Alex? You game?" Brayden has worked his way into our tight circle, palming a set of darts in both hands.

"Shouldn't you be resting that thing?" I say, motioning to his right arm.

He smirks.

"I'll throw lefty. Make it more even for you."

I laugh through my last bite. Sadly, he's not wrong. I'm shit at darts. I don't get the fine motor control of it all. If I could fling the things at the board the way I throw screwdrivers into the dirt back home, I might have something. But the precise flick of the wrist? That skill is lost on me. But I'm sure as hell not backing down from him in front of Nikki. I can't figure out why she's willing to entertain this asshole again.

"Sure, Brayden. Let's do this," I say, taking the darts from his right hand and feeling the weight in my palm.

Nikki raises a brow as she slides from her stool to join us. "I'm not so sure this is the way to make him jealous," she whispers at my side. She's grabbed both of our beers, which is good because odds are I'm going to need to drink after Brayden embarrasses me.

"Yeah, I know. Just . . . be my good luck charm. He'll hate that. And let's face it, I need one." I grimace at her as I spin around to walk backward. Her head tilts with a certain sense of pity because I think she knows I mean that in a broader sense. I need luck for a lot of things.

Nikki slides into one of the high tops by the pool tables and the dart machines. Brayden sets up our game while I take a few practice throws on the board next to us. My first attempt scores a seven, and the next two in the double lines.

"Hey, okay," I say, winking at Nikki as I spin around to retrieve my darts.

"I'm impressed you hit the board," she says through her raspy laugh.

"Me, too," Brayden adds. Damn, I almost forgot he was here. But isn't he the point? Nikki and he high five at my expense and I force my smile to stay wide, then wind up to take one more practice throw. This time I send the dart into the men's room door.

"Good thing that was closed," Brayden says.

"Good thing that was closed," I repeat in that pouty child voice I usually only reserve for hitting work with my dad.

And fuck, now I'm thinking about my dad. And Brayden's relationship with my dad's girlfriend. And his smug face. Both of their smug faces. Everyone's *smug face!*

"Let's go," I say, yanking my dart from the well-graffitied Patty's bathroom door. One of the Tiff hockey players pushes through a second later, and I glance over my shoulder to take in his massive body.

"I don't know that the dart would have stood a chance," Nikki jokes. I shrug, though that was funny and I think she was only trying to shift the jokes to not be at my expense.

"You ready, slugger?" Brayden says, baiting me. I gnash my molars but force a smile.

"You first," I say.

Brayden lines up, weight on his front foot as his long arm reaches practically half the distance to the board. He squints and flexes his wrist, then turns his gaze to me.

"Little wager?"

I shrug.

"Depends," I say. I don't really have cash to drop to this fool tonight.

"Winner gets to dance with Nikki to the song of her choice," he says.

I glance to my friend in time to catch her spitting out her sip of beer. She waves her hand. "Absolutely not—"

"Deal," I agree, ignoring her wishes completely.

Dammit!

I *am* an asshole.

I will myself to take it back. To toss the damn darts on the table and walk away. Go back to the pub side with Cutter and Cole. Hell, go home!

"Deal," Brayden says.

I don't say a word. I simply step to the side and watch him knock down three twenties in a row. I swear, the only reason he skipped the bullseye was to drag this out and watch me squirm.

He plucks his darts from the board, then steps to the side with a wave of his hand.

"You're up, sport."

I glare at him as he walks by, a deep chuckle emanating from his throat that I think is just for me.

"What's with the nicknames?"

Brayden rocks back a step and leans in, his eyes glancing to Nikki briefly, then back to me.

"My cousin told me your dad calls you by them." His lip ticks up on one side, and I'd swear I smell smoke pouring from his breath like some sort of demon. Fucking asshole.

"You know what?" I suck my lips in tight and glance to Nikki, who is sitting with her arms crossed over her chest, clearly pissed that I let this go this far. That I am about to make her a bet. That's not what friends do to friends. And it's not what I do to Nik.

I toss the darts on the table and turn to look Brayden in the eyes.

"I'm out." I wipe my hands of him, literally, and saunter back to the table where Cole and Cutter are looking on. I have a keen feeling my teammate is filling him in on the backstory to the extent he knows it.

I slide back onto my stool and top off my beer with what's left in the pitcher.

"Hey," Cutter says, reaching over the table toward me with a fist. I stare at it for a few seconds then pound it with my own.

"It's not easy being the bigger man," he says, and I smile to myself as I take a long sip from my beer.

"Thanks," I say with a nod as I put the mug back down.

"It pays off, though," Cutter adds, leaning in and glancing over my shoulder.

I spin around to see Nikki making her way back to us, her walk slow and purposeful. She's swaying her hips exaggeratingly, and I smile on one side. She's cute when she's trying to cheer me up. I also wouldn't hold it against her if she hauled back and socked me in the jaw for that little display back there.

"I told Brayden I got to pick the winner," she says, sliding her now empty mug on the table before taking my hand.

"You sure I deserve to win anything?"

I let her lead me out to the dance floor where some of the older folks are two-stepping. I'm not very good at this type of dancing, but maybe I deserve to fumble my way around the dance floor as punishment.

I thread my fingers with Nikki's and she turns into me, my hand resting at her hip. I look down to study my feet as I take a deep breath, but Nikki reaches for my chin and tips my gaze back up to hers.

"Uh uh," she says.

My brow pulls in.

"Deal was, I pick the song," she says, a devious smirk slowly taking up the real estate of her face.

Just then, the music changes over to the next pick, and the rawest, nastiest, thrasher-fest of a metal song pours out of Patty's speakers. Nikki holds up her pinky and index finger then begins to head bang, her beanie flopping to the floor while her wild hair flings around her face.

My head falls back as I howl with laughter, then join my friend for the world's smallest mosh pit. I even let her rush at me and smash into my ribs a few times before catching her on the last one and steadying our worlds for a beat.

"You're going to hurt yourself," I laugh out.

She shakes her head then brings her hands up, pushing her fingertips into her temples. She grimaces but turns it into a relenting smile, finally resting both hands on my shoulders.

"Yeah, alright. That was maybe a bit much."

I rock us to whatever beat I can find, the floor cleared from the audio assault Nikki unleashed.

"I can't believe that was even an option on the juke-box," I say through a soft laugh.

Nikki steps in close, her cheek resting on the center of my chest, and I drop my hands down to her waist.

"I know all the deep cuts on that thing," she says.

"Of course you do."

Eventually, her thrasher song plays out and shifts back into a slow country song. I don't budge, and she seems perfectly content staying right where we are.

"That was sure weird," an older man says as he brings his wife back onto the dance floor. He glances to the head of my best friend, which is still tucked against my chest.

"It's always weird," I tell him, earning me a quick poke in the ribs.

"Ahh, hey!" I laugh out as I arch from her tickle attack.

"That's still not fair," I say, running my hands around her waist to the small of her back. I slip them under her sweatshirt, expecting to feel the fabric of a T-shirt under-neath, but instead, my palms meet bare skin. Her body stiffens, and for a blip, I pause our rocking motion.

"Sorry," I say as I start to pull them away.

"No, don't," she says, shifting her head so her chin is propped on my chest. "It's nice."

Her eyes blink slowly, and my lungs fill with this fluttering sensation like I've been drugged. I nod softly then drop my lips to her forehead. Her eyes close and a tranquil smile pulls at the sides of her mouth.

"I bet Brayden's jealous," she says.

I don't bother looking. I'm sure he is. In fact, he's probably plotting my demise at this very moment. But I don't care about Brayden right now. I care about this girl right here, and the sudden massive confusion rattling around my head over how I feel and what I'm going to do about it.

"Let him," I say.

Let him.

Let . . . me.

nikki

I MAY SKIP CLASS SOMETIMES. Okay, I may skip accounting constantly. But, I've never sat out an entire day from anything in my life. Usually, I skip the thing I'm *supposed* to do because there's something I'd *rather* do.

But yesterday? I did nothing. Literally. Nothing.

I couldn't. I woke up with this strange urge to vomit, sat up, felt my world spin, then instantly laid back down. Omar had to cover my floor meeting with my residents, which, well, that was a win. The floor meetings are mandatory and nobody wants to be there. This month is a door decorating contest for a ten-dollar food hall gift card. I can all but guarantee the only girl who has a white board on her door on which she sarcastically writes THIS IS MY (FILL IN THE MONTH) DECORATION ENTRY will be the winner. She's the only one who participates.

The weird thing is, I couldn't stand the thought of music in my ears yesterday. I tried, both with my headphones and without. But the sound only made my head feel worse—throbbing and swirling, with nothing good to show for it.

Alex kept offering to come over and take care of me, which I wanted desperately, especially after our night at Patty's. I'm even more confused about my situation than I was before. But also, I'm kind of freaked out about my head. And the last thing I want to do is freak Alex out. He has enough on his plate without worrying about me having a dizzy spell or two. Besides, I woke up normal today. So I'm sure it was a bug.

But the fact the mix I made last week now sounds completely fucked up has me concerned. I haven't changed a thing, and looking at the settings proves it visually. Why it doesn't *sound* right is a mystery.

I drop my headphones to my neck and close my laptop at the feel of my phone vibrating. I pull it out of my pocket to see my mom calling, and my stomach tightens because as close as me and her are, she doesn't call much. This could only mean one thing.

"Hey, Mom."

"Did you know about Senior and Marie?" Senior is Alex's dad. That's how Mom and I keep them straight. She's known them both since high school, so I'm sure this news has her in a tizzy.

I sigh.

"*¡Mija!* How come you didn't tell me?"

I knew she would fly right to this.

"Because I was being there for Alex, and he said Marie was working through things and would tell you on her own time." I fail to mention that Alex only told me a few days ago. Last thing I need is my mom exploring why Alex would keep it a secret too.

"Okay, well. It's good he has you. He must be really upset. This is such a surprise. They were—" She stops there and simply sighs out a sob.

This is my mom. And I am positive this is why Marie waited to tell her until she was absolutely ready for Julianne Thomas's emotional sympathy. It's why my mom can't watch Hallmark movies. She takes everything to heart—*deeply* to heart.

"He's doing all right, but he's pretty upset with Senior." I plop my phone on my bed and turn it to speaker so I can change for Alex's game while my mom continues to share her emotional journey.

"Talk about upset! Marie is letting him off easy, in my opinion. And I told her we are putting her up on all the dating sites. Right now. Forget this trial separation business. There's no three strikes for this. It's one strike. Right? Isn't that how it goes?"

I sigh quietly to myself, not wanting her to hear me.

"Yes, Mama." I know when it's time to use my sweet voice. And when to tell her she's right. I'll let her go on for a while. Maybe getting it out of her system with me will save Marie from having to deal with it.

"I agree," I add in, setting off a new rant. She's picking up steam and shifting to the angry side. This version of her will be more beneficial to Marie.

I wiggle out of the oversized T-shirt I've lived in for the

past two days and tip over my basket of clean laundry, cursing myself for never putting stuff away. Most of my shirts are wrinkled, but the jersey Alex gave me from his freshman year isn't too bad. I slip on my snug black hoodie and then toss the jersey over it. The wind is very much present today, so I'm going to want to have that hood up. Plus, since I'm going to the game alone, this means I won't have to talk to anyone. The hoodie is a sure-fire way of securing introvert status.

I slip on my jeans and sneakers, then feel around my crumpled blankets for my Tiff baseball cap. I pull my hair through the back then pull the hoodie up over the top.

"Mama? Hey, I . . ." She doesn't seem to hear me, so I pop my earbuds in and let her continue to vent as I gather up my keys and wallet, then head out for Alex's game.

My mom manages to slip through three complete stages of friendship sympathy during my walk to the stadium—grief, anger, and now party planning.

"I'm not sure Marie is ready for a girls' night just yet, but you probably know best," I say, showing my student ID to the security officer. He waves me through, and I drop my cell phone in the bin as I pass through the metal detector. I pick it up on the other side, my mom none the wiser.

"Hey, Mom?" I manage to catch her between breaths.

"Yes, baby."

"I have to get to Alex's game. So I need to go. But can you send me our insurance info? I need to make an appointment—"

"Nikki Thomas, are you pregnant?" she shouts into my ear. I'm glad I don't feel the way I did yesterday. That shrill question would have busted my ear drum.

"Jesus, Ma! No, I'm not. I have an earache. I just need to go to student health. It's fine." I scan the seats, which are half-filled because it's opening day. The only time this place is full is for concerts and playoffs.

"Okay, but you better not get pregnant!"

I laugh because this is how the sex talk with my mom started when I was twelve. There was no easing me into birds and bees, which, face it, I had already picked up the details from classmates on the playground. My mom went right to the scare tactics—teenage pregnancy risks, how it affects college attendance, graduation rates, future employment. I dared to bring up Aunt Mara, who had my cousin Sonia at sixteen. That's when I learned about how hard Mara worked to get where she is—owning her own boutique in Iowa City. I'll admit it gave me good perspective, but also—maybe would have been nice to get the speech about two people being in love and waiting. That's the version Alex got. We compared notes.

"I'll text you a picture of the card. Tell me how it goes at the appointment. You know I worry," she says.

"Oh, *I know.*"

I hear her grumble but she relents and says she loves me before ending the call.

I pull my earbuds out and tuck them in my case and then my pocket, and scan the stadium for Alicia. As I feared, she's in the same seat as last time—*my* seat. I could run and hide as I did before or suck it up and play nice. Since this is where I've sat for every home game over the last three years, I decide Alex knowing where to find me is more important than my ego, so I push my phone in my back pocket and take a deep breath.

"Hey, got room for one more?" I ask, noting that she's brought two friends with her. They're all taking selfies right now.

"Yeah, down there," Alicia says, nodding to the seat that puts two people between us.

"Thanks," I say, begrudgingly. She's in *my* seat, but I promised I'd be nice. And Alex is stressed today. He'll find me three feet in another direction.

I keep my hoodie up until it's time to stand for the national anthem. I slip it off and pull my hat from my head and stare at my favorite player on the field. His hands fidget with his hat behind his back, and I can tell he's nervous. This isn't my normal Alex.

While my seatmates giggle through the ceremonial first pitch and group together to take more selfies with the field in the background, I tuck my hair through my hat again and leave the hoodie down for now so Alex can spot me. He's stretching just outside the dugout, pulling his legs up to get loose. Once he's still, punching his fist into the pocket of his mitt, the brim of his hat tips up and I can tell he's found me. I nod, and he nods back. I sink into my seat and prop one foot on the cupholder to my right as I seriously consider moving down an extra seat or two.

Be nice, he said.

Our guys take the field, which means, for now, I can relax. Fielding has never been a worry, as he proves by making a diving stop and managing to throw the runner out from his knees.

"Wow!" one of Alicia's friends says, clapping. I smirk, part of me proud of her for noticing and acknowledging it.

"I told you he was good," Alicia adds.

I pop my mouth open but stop short of speaking actual words.

Be nice.

I sit back instead, comfortable enough in my own knowledge that Alicia has never actually seen him play.

The inning ends with a line drive to Alex that he catches with ease then tosses to our second baseman as they jog off the field. I hold my breath for the next test. I noticed Alex is slotted to bat sixth, which isn't the usual lead-off he's used to. I'm sure it's to take pressure off of him, but also, I know Alex. This move does nothing but add to his pressure, his feeling of failure.

"Come on, Alex," I mutter quietly.

"You come to a lot of games?" the girl next to me asks.

I meet her gaze, skepticism in my eyes. She's being friendly, I remind myself.

"Quite a few," I say. *All of them.*

"This is my first one. I'm so excited. Alicia used to date him, number five?" She points to Alex who is taking warm-up swings just outside the dugout.

"Is that right? Wow, lucky girl," I say, doing my best to mask my natural sarcasm.

"I think they still like each other," she says, leaning over and whispering to me.

I nod and hold my mouth in the *ah* position while the jealousy soup boils in my gut. Thankfully, our first batter is announced, so I turn my focus back to the field and finger the strings of my hoodie while I mentally debate putting up my fleece forcefield.

Edwin is DHing, which Alex expected. He's also in the four-hole, which I guess he's earned. The guy can hit. But seeing his name loom large has got to be getting into Alex's head.

Our lead-off hitter walks, and our number two, Cole, gets hit by a pitch.

"Oww!" my seatmate says, cupping her mouth. I'll give her this, at least she's really watching. Alicia and her friend right next to her are scrolling through socials.

"They get hit a lot. They can take it," I say, feeling like educating her a little.

"Really? They don't have pads?"

I chuckle.

"No, they aren't like hockey or football players."

She nods, her face serious. *Oh boy.*

Our third batter gets on with a single, loading the bases for Edwin. When the announcer introduces him, the stadium roars with anticipation, partly because the bases are juiced and part due to the hype that Edwin comes with. He was pretty flashy in high school. Let's see if that translates to college pitching.

The first pitch comes in at ninety-nine (*thank you, speed*

gun guy). Edwin swings through it like he's wielding a sword and merely tops the ball, sending it foul. The guys in the dugout grow rowdy, Alex joining them as they chirp and try to get into the pitcher's head. It's effective, as the next pitch is in the dirt.

My thumbnail finds its way between my teeth, and I'm not sure whether I'm rooting for Edwin to fail or succeed right now. It becomes abundantly clear, though, as the next pitch comes in, and he sends it screaming over the left field scoreboard. Everyone—Alicia included—gets to their feet, cheering. But I'm glued in place, my focus on Alex as he does his best to rally for his team, to congratulate the guy he sees as a threat. And now he has to clear his head and wait his turn.

"That was amazing!" the girl next to me says.

"*Mmm*, it was," I say, forcing a smile.

"Do you know him?" She nods to the field where everyone is patting Edwin on the helmet.

"Not really," I say. "I'm friends with Alex."

She shifts in her seat, twisting and dropping her sunglasses down her nose as if she didn't see me fully before.

"You," she says, waggling her finger at me. "You must be Nikki."

"I am, indeed," I say with a tight-lipped smile.

I linger on her gaze for a few seconds, waiting for her to introduce herself, but she never does. And her attention shifts to the girl sitting to her left. I'm pretty sure this baseball education session is done.

Our catcher bats fifth and pops out to first base. The fact that Alex is up with nobody on and no risk of being the third out gives me some comfort. And at least Alicia is paying enough attention to realize he's up. She gets to her feet and cups her mouth, screaming his name. I know he can't hear her, but I promised I'd be nice, so I'll let her keep at it. Maybe somehow he will feel everyone behind him. Most of the fans here don't know he had a rough fall.

He steps in, digging his back foot in as he always does and engaging his hips with a few quick jolts like a wind-up getting ready to be cut loose. I sit forward and ball my hands together, picking at the corner of my thumbnail.

Come on, Alex.

I keep my support internal, willing it to him through our bond. As his shoulders relax and the bat bobs on his shoulder, I grow confident. He looks ready. It's a carbon copy of every at bat he's had over the last three years. Nothing is off, at least not that I can tell.

I swallow as the pitch comes, and it zips in for a questionable first strike.

"That seemed outside," I mumble. I don't bother glancing to my left. I don't care if they can hear me. Or aren't listening to me.

Alex digs in again and takes a deep breath, his shoulders dropping as he readies his stance. I'm betting on a curveball. It seems so is Alex as he sits back and swings through one, topping the ball and spinning it foul into his dugout.

I dig my nails into my palm.

"You got this," I say, my voice growing louder.

There's a shift in his stance now, and when he lets out his breath to relax, his shoulders remain tense. He's in the box, but there's no digging. He's off-balance. Not ready. And when he swings through the third strike, not even close to fouling off the slider, I feel sick.

"Shit," I say, nice and loud this time.

"He'll get it next time," Alicia says, still on her feet and clapping.

I smile at her, though she never looks. At least I can appreciate that she's in his corner—in her own way.

The game drags on, and by the seventh inning and nearing three hours, Alicia and her friends have bailed. I move back to my favorite seat, propping my feet on the back of the seat in front of me, and cup my knees with my sweaty palms. It's pretty chilly out, the sun dropping in the afternoon and the breeze picking up. But somehow, my hands are sweating. Alex has struck out twice and flied out once. He has one more at bat coming up, and he needs this. It doesn't matter that we're up five to one. He won't focus on the win, and not because he's being a selfish player. He'll focus on his failures because this is his dream.

I sit forward after we get the last outs of the seventh and head into the eighth, my eyes scanning the dugout for Alex. He should be getting his helmet on, slipping on his batting gloves, but I don't spot him.

Oh no. No, no, no!

The announcer begins to say it a second after the reality hits me.

"Batting for Alex Mendoza is number eighteen, Patrick Burnes."

No!

I get to my feet, check my pockets to make sure nothing's dropped, and head down to the clubhouse where I camp outside the door. I don't care how the game plays out, and I hear enough from this spot to know that Patrick does well, hitting a single and managing to steal second. I close my eyes through the rest of the game, hoping my friend can feel me somehow. I want to hug him. I want to charge through these doors and march into that dugout and grab his coach by the collar and tell him he's not helping! But that wouldn't be helping either.

So I sit. And the game finishes. And after every other player has left, mine comes shuffling through the door, his eye black smeared from tears. The only thing I have to offer is my arms, my heart, my love. So I give it to him. I let him ruin the jersey he gave me by bawling into my shoulder and smearing eye black on the white fabric. I grasp the back of his dirty, sweaty neck and try not to think about the dried blood on his elbow from the amazing stops he made today.

None of the good will matter to him right now because all he can focus on is the bad.

"You want to stay over tonight?" I ask, knowing he's definitely not up for hanging with the guys. He didn't even bother to shower in the clubhouse.

He sniffles and nods.

"Yeah. Just let me . . . shower. Mind coming with me and waiting?"

I shake my head, my gaze locked on his glossy eyes.

"Never," I say, threading my hand with his and making the slow, melancholy march to the parking lot.

**8 /
alex**

"SORRY I CAN'T STAY at your place. Hazard of the job," Nik says, piling her pillows along the wall and turning her laptop to face us on her desk.

"I don't mind it here, actually. No dudes screaming obscene shit up and down the stairs. Other than the fact I have to go up one floor to pee, I'm comfortable."

I kick my shoes off and crawl into her bed, glad I put on my sweats and old high school hoodie. Something about being wrapped up in warm, worn-out clothes feels right for wallowing.

"Okay, do we want to relive our youth or watch something new?" She toggles her computer between two screens, one with our favorite show from fifth grade where a family of nine juggles life in New York City—super practical. The other option is a war movie, which feels dismal.

"Maybe just put on the hockey game?" I shrug, and she tilts her head back in laughter.

"Okay, Mr. Hockey Players Get Everything Around

Here. I'll put the Tiff game on. You know the student stream is shitty though, right?" She clicks a few links and soon the sound of blades on ice, grunting, and fans echoing in our arena takes over as white noise.

"I don't really need to watch. I just like to listen. And maybe I'll get some tips on confidence from Cutter. That guy's never in a slump." I sink down so my neck is bent and clutch Nikki's giant stuffed strawberry to my chest.

"Cutter can't hit a fastball," she retorts, sinking down next to me, our shoulders touching.

"Ha! Neither can I."

Nikki smacks my chest with her heart pillow and I grunt, though it didn't really hurt. She rolls to her side and points at me.

"Rule number one—no negative talk tonight." She lifts her brows and awaits my agreement. I know better than to refuse.

"Fair rule. Okay, I'll try." And I will try. But I feel pretty low right now. And I'm not sure how to stop this cycle that's following me into the batter's box.

Nikki picks up my arm and slides against my chest. I wrap my arm around her back and hold her shoulder, the same warmth I felt when we danced heating my palm. I tuck my chin, my view of her smoothed-back hair, her eyelashes, the round tip of her nose, and pouty upper lip. Her nose and cheeks are peppered with faint freckles that nobody would notice unless they were this close to her. And for some reason, the thought of anyone else being *this* close makes my chest squeeze.

"I was nice today," she says, her eyes flitting up to meet my gaze. I'm surprisingly fine with her catching me looking at her. I squint one eye.

"Being nice is generally a good thing," I say with a chuckle.

"No, I mean"—Her gaze drops and she moves her hand up to rest between my ribs. My insides tremble and tighten, and not because I'm ticklish. She lets out a heavy sigh before looking up again—"I was nice to Alicia."

"Oh." I'd honestly forgotten Alicia came. For a tiny second before the game started I noted it, but mostly because I wanted to tell Nikki she was wrong. Now, though, proving Nikki wrong feels pointless. And beyond that, mean.

"Well, thanks for being nice. I doubt she'll be back." Alicia is a lot like Brayden. Actually, maybe the two of them should hook up. They can sit next to each other and stare at their phones, looking at themselves.

"I don't know. She seems like a pretty big Alex Mendoza fan." Nikki's mouth settles into a lopsided smile, and I get the feeling she's jealous. I've always thought that to be the case on some level, but more because she and I are close, and anytime someone else pushes their way into our bubble things feel unbalanced. But now, I'm starting to think she might have a different kind of jealousy. A kind that isn't just for friends.

I swallow the dryness in my throat and move my thumb along her bare shoulder. Her body beats with a sudden breath as her lips part. My gaze dips to the upturn of her top lip, but only for a second. Upon reflection, sweatpants were maybe *not* the best idea.

"You know I'm not getting back with Alicia, right?" I hold her stare as we both take a deep, slow breath.

"Okay," she says, her raspy voice coming through. She gets this way when she's tired. Or drunk. Or after a concert at which she's been shouting lyrics for two hours straight.

Some of her hair has slipped from behind her ear and it crosses her forehead. I reach across and sweep it back in place, then let my hand linger along her cheek. My thumb caresses the curve of her cheekbone and she turns her head slightly, leaning into my touch as she blinks slowly and sighs.

"Are you trying to make me blush, Alex Mendoza?"

"How so?" I curl my fingers and run my knuckles along her jawline. I'm crossing boundaries right now, and I know better. But I can't seem to stop.

"You're staring at me, and it's—"

"Weird?" I quirk a brow, wondering if she'll remember our kiss and my incredibly lame response.

She breathes out a tiny laugh and her mouth curves against my fingers.

"Yeah, weird," she says, her eyes settling on mine.

Her body is so still, I think she may be holding her breath. I'm definitely guarding mine. No sudden movements. Nothing to disturb this fragile ecosystem. Only me and Nik and the line that I'm casually moving further and further from safe.

My gaze dips to her mouth again as I inch my thumb along her lips. She exhales a soft breath, her dark lashes kissing the tops of her cheeks as her eyes close. There are plenty of times I've wanted to kiss my best friend, including the time we were coaxed into it our freshman year. I've always been able to stop myself when we're alone, but I'm starting to wonder why?

Why stop?

Because what if . . .

"Was it weird?" she says, her lips moving softly against my thumb. She pulls them together and presses a soft kiss to the side of my hand.

I *feel* it.

I open my mouth but pause, drawing in a breath, unable to take my eyes off her inviting lips, her beautiful brown eyes, the way her lashes somehow act like dark angel wings.

"Well?"

A tinge of nervousness vibrates her voice, so I ease my lips into a soft smile and tilt my head, sliding down lower on the bed so we're closer to the same level. She shifts to lay on her side so we're facing, and her hands gather the strings of my hoodie into two fists.

I smirk.

"It was weird only because that's not how I ever pictured it," I say.

She draws in a sharp breath, then bites her bottom lip. I tug it free, mostly to have an excuse to leave my thumb on her mouth for longer. It's soft. Plump. Intoxicating.

"You imagined kissing me?"

I chuckle softly and nod my forehead toward hers, nearly touching her.

"All. The damn. Time," I admit.

Her cheeks flush, and being so close, and the fact she's wearing her oversized Van Halen T-shirt that falls off her shoulder and slings low at the neck, I can see that much of her upper body is pink.

"You ever think about it?" I have my suspicions, but also, it's Nikki. When you're as close as the two of us, sometimes it's hard to read signs. I've always thought she felt something more, but also—*it's Nikki.*

She drops her gaze and tucks her chin, her forehead touching my collarbone as she laughs lightly.

"You have no idea, Alex Mendoza."

I nudge her chin back with my fingertips and hold her gaze. She doesn't blink. Neither do I. I don't want to miss anything.

"Maybe it was weird because everyone was staring at us."

"*Mmm,* yeah. That part"—she chuckles—"was definitely weird."

"Like, I think I remember someone shouting *chug, chug, chug* in the background," I say, and we both laugh. Nervously.

"You know, we could try again. For scientific purposes. Without the crowd. So we know for sure, I mean. You know . . . if kissing me is . . . *weird.*"

My smile softens and my tongue peeks out from

between my teeth and bottom lip. My skin buzzes with the urge to drop all caution. To go for it.

"For science, *hmm?*" Nikki hums.

I nod.

"Yeah," I say, my mouth now close enough to hers that it brushes against her bottom lip as I speak.

"For the record, Alex," she says, taking a nip at my upper lip between words. My chest ignites, and my body shifts automatically, so I'm lying on top of her, caging her head between my forearms. I pull back enough to look her in her eyes, sweeping her hair back and cupping her face. She's always been beautiful.

"I never thought it was weird," she says, and my smile crawls across my mouth.

I close my eyes and shake my head, then waste no more precious time. I cover her mouth with mine, sucking her top lip in, fighting the urge to bite it. That lip. *Damn, that lip!* More than her curves in those tight jeans, I have spent years looking at the upturned lip next to me in the passenger seat.

While I'm holding back, Nikki's teeth graze along my lower lip, tugging my skin as her tongue passes over it.

"Gah!" I let out, peppering her lips with kisses as laughter sets in.

"What?" She giggles.

"This! It isn't weird at all. It's so fucking *not* weird," I say, diving in for more.

Her mouth opens, deepening our kiss, and I allow my tongue to explore all of her. She bends her knee against my hip, and I doubt there's a chance she isn't feeling what she's doing to me. When her hips lift, I know she is.

"Nicole Jasmine Thomas," I utter softly in her ear as I make my way down the curve of her neck. She breathes out a short laugh that quickly melts into a whimper.

"You're going to have to tell me when," I say, my teeth tugging at the collar of her T-shirt.

"When?" she breathes out, arching her back. *Is this permission?*

I swallow hard and kiss her bare shoulder, then the divot along her throat.

"When to stop," I say, grabbing the center of her collar with my teeth and tugging it lower. She's dressed for bed. And I've slept with her enough—*sleeping*—to know she takes her bra off the minute she has a chance.

"And if I don't?" she says, sinking her teeth into my neck. I think she might actually leave a mark. I *hope* she does.

I halt my kisses and stare at the tiny heart-shaped mole on the center of her collarbone. I make a wish on it as if it's a star. *Please don't fuck up this friendship.*

"Then I won't," I say, dragging my hand down the side of her body and gripping her thigh, pulling her leg up even more so I can sink into her. So she can feel what she does to me.

I thread my fingers through hers on one side, holding her hand against the bed as we kiss while my other hand glides up her waist, under her T-shirt and to the bottom curve of her breast. It's taking all the willpower I have to slow down, to savor every first. And when Nikki moans into my mouth, arching her back, basically begging my hand to keep trailing upward, I give in.

My fingertips graze the hard peak of her nipple, and I run my thumb over it next, in circles until I feel her breathing pick up with want. I squeeze the hard peak between my thumb and index finger, rolling it to ease her need. Her hips buck up, pressing her body into my hard cock. She's wearing those tiny little sleep shorts, the ones that look like boxers, and I want to rip them off.

Tugging her shirt up to expose her tits, I drop my mouth to the one I've now rolled into a raw bright pink with my hand, soothing it with my tongue.

"Oh, my God!" Nikki pants. I flick the hard tip with my tongue, feeling her body quiver every time I do. I suck it in and hold it between my teeth as she writhes beneath me, her hands deep in my hair, grabbing fists full.

I move to the other one, flicking again, puckering it with my lips then sucking it into my mouth so my teeth can graze the soft pink tip.

"You taste so fucking good, Nik. I never want to stop tasting you. All of you," I say, leading her to what I really want.

"Yes," she moans, her hands dropping to my shoulders as she pushes me lower.

I sit up, straddling her and pulling her T-shirt over her head, tossing it to the floor, then pause for just a breath to admire her. My hands roam over her shoulders, my fingers painting down her tits, my fingers curling to scratch along her hard nipples. All the while her hips wiggle beneath me.

When she reaches for the bottom of my hoodie, I take her direction and pull it over my head, sending it to the floor with her concert shirt. Her palms flatten on my stomach, her fingers taking their time to trace along my muscles. Every damn crunch in that gym was worth this moment right now. Her palms trail up my chest, then over my pecs. I drop down, kissing her and allowing her time to touch my back, and my hips. And then her palm drops to my massive hard-on, cupping it and running her thumb along the length through my sweatpants.

"Oh, fuck!" I groan, tucking my mouth in the crook of her neck.

I lick my way down her body, stopping to taste her nipples one more time before continuing down her body, between her ribs, to her belly button. The small stud she's had since we were teenagers looks a whole lot different like this, and I flick it with my tongue.

"I told you that was sexy," she says, teasing me for calling it dumb when we were sixteen.

I kiss her belly.

"You were right, Nik. This"—I pause to flick it again with my tongue—"is very sexy."

"Oh," she says, her voice breathy and raw.

I curl my fingers into the band of her sleep shorts and slide them down her body, stopping to kiss the white silk band of her panties that cuts across her abdomen. She lifts her hips and I roll her shorts down more, sliding them over her curves as I sit up on my knees to let her slip her legs out one at a time.

She's trembling, and I'm sure she's nervous. This step is momentous. It's irreversible. It will change everything. She's revealing herself to me, for the first time in our lives. *To know someone so well and then to see them bare, vulnerable.*

Mine.

"Goddamn, Nik." I bite my thumbnail as I take her in.

She tucks her chin against her shoulder, demure. Shy. Her leg comes up, knee bending and tucking in to hide her modesty.

"Yeah?" she asks, and it isn't a play. She isn't being coy. She's worried too.

I nod slowly and lift her leg to my side as my eyes hold hers hostage.

"Yeah, Nikki. Fucking beautiful," I say, closing my eyes and kissing the inside of her knee. "Very much yeah."

I lower her leg and press both palms on her knees, carefully reaching behind her legs until I have her secure enough to help her to the edge of the bed, which isn't far. My feet find the floor and I lift her hips, pulling her gently by the legs until she's trapped at the edge of her mattress, her legs under my control, her pussy mine to taste.

"Are we stopping?" I ask, hoping she says no. She shakes her head and I drop to my knees, spreading her legs wide, the thin silk band that covers her pussy hiding very little. She's so swollen, so ready to be tasted.

That friend line? Fucking obliterated.

I hook my finger around the thin strip that hides

nothing and allow my knuckle to press into her swollen pussy. Her knees close around me, and I chuckle.

"Ah ah ah, princess. Keep those legs open," I command. She relaxes, and her legs spread more, giving me more.

"Fuck," I mutter, licking my lips as I pull the center strip of her panties to the side. Leaning in, I first taste her with the tip of my tongue, taking languid strokes along her center and pausing to press my tongue against the most sensitive spot. Her hips buck, so I reach up with my hand and press down on her abdomen, lowering her and pinning her to the edge of the bed.

I torture her with slow glides of my tongue for several minutes, until she's breathing as if she ran a marathon. I can feel the force of her pelvis working to push up against my hand. I sit up, my mouth leaving her only for a moment so I can tug her panties down her hips and over her ass. She lifts, then allows me to bring her legs over my shoulder to pull her panties away completely. She's less shy now, and allows me to shift her legs back, spreading them wide so I can taste all of her.

I lap her up and she begins to moan, her hips circling while I suckle in her swollen pink center. My hand trails from her hip to her abdomen, my fingertips following the thin trail of hair that leads to her perfect pussy. Her skin is so soft. Her taste sweet, like a tonic of sugar and lavender.

When my hand sinks between her legs, I dip a finger inside of her, hooking it just enough to press where she can feel the most pleasure.

"Oh, my God, Alex!" She covers her face with her forearm and arches her back as I move my finger in and out of her.

"Do you like this, Nikki?"

"Uh huh," she whines.

I add a second finger, moving them in and out as I continue to suck the top of her pussy, my hand covered in her wetness. I'm so hard, it's difficult not to be selfish. I want to drive my dick inside of her right now, but also, more than anything, I want to see her come because of me. I want to see what her face looks like when I give her pleasure. I want to taste every last drop.

"Can I make you come, Nikki?" I slow my hand and she whimpers, nodding.

"Then I need to see your face."

Her mouth opens, her bottom lip trembling as she lifts her head so her eyes meet mine.

"Look what I do to you," I say, dropping my chin and licking her up.

"Uh huh," she cries.

"Do you like it when my tongue tastes your pussy?" Words I've maybe fantasized about saying to her fall from my mouth with ease. I want to say so much more, but I'll hold back for now.

"Yes, Alex. Very much," she whimpers.

"Can you come on my tongue?" I flick her skin once, then lift my head to meet her eyes.

She nods, then brings her fist to her mouth, biting her knuckle. The way I have her nearly undone makes me smile. I suck her raw center into my mouth and punish it with my tongue while my fingers work in and out. Her hips buck, the rhythm growing faster, and I'm not sure who is driving the speed—me or her.

Her thighs start to close in on me and I know she's close.

"Leave those open, baby. I want you to take it all," I say, and she shakes, forcing her legs to splay.

Pressing my thumb down on the top of her pussy, I let my tongue push in and out of her until I feel her lower body begin to tremble.

"Oh, Alex!" She's not quiet at all, and I love it.

"That's it," I praise, feeling her start to convulse. Her pussy flexes around my tongue then squeezes, and I lick every drop that escapes her, consuming her.

When her hands fall to her sides and her legs go slack, I feel satisfied that I've drained every last wave of pleasure from her core. I sit back on my heels and breathe her in, reaching into my sweatpants and fisting my cock for relief.

Nikki lifts herself up on her elbows, her eyes dipping to the edge of the mattress. She bites her lower lip.

"It's only fair," she says.

"Oh, thank God," I say, getting to my feet and working my sweats down my legs at record speed.

Nikki scoots to the end of the bed, sitting up and wrapping her hand around mine where I'm holding myself.

"Let me get this," she says, a devilish flirtation to her tone.

I relent and let go, my hands moving to caress her face, to slide the loose hairs from her eyes and mouth, to gather her hair in one hand, vowing to let her lead.

Her eyes flutter up to me just as she sticks out her tongue and rests the tip of my dick on it. *I'm in fucking trouble.*

With the slightest grin on her lips, she closes them around my shaft and slowly takes me in, inch by inch, her eyes never leaving mine. I pull her hair tighter, relaxing when I expect her to wince. She moans instead, so I give her head a little push as her mouth slides down my cock again.

I'm not a giant, but I'm definitely not small. And I don't want to hurt her. But also, the idea of watching her swallow my cum has me on the very edge, so whatever pain this may cause will be brief. I move my hips slowly at first, fucking her mouth. She braces herself with her hands on my hips, never once resisting. I push in deeper, and when I pull out, she sucks my tip, which pushes me over the edge.

"Oh, fuck, Nik. I'm going to come," I warn her. She wraps her hand around my base and slides her mouth around my cock, the sound of her lips smacking, her throat being pushed to the limit, the tiny whimper that leaves her body every time she takes me.

I'm no use against these forces, and I fill her mouth with my cum, pumping until I'm sure she's taken it all. My head falls back and I exhale, my body covered in a sheen of sweat. How is she so perfect still? I instantly consider spoiling her next time.

Next time.

There *will* be a next time.

I help her wipe her chin, then coax her back in bed so she's lying flat and caged beneath me. I press a kiss to her forehead, then stop to look into her eyes. I can't pull myself away, and I know it's getting awkward the longer I stare into her without words, but I can't believe what I've been missing.

"For the record," I say, dropping a soft kiss to her lips. "Not weird at all."

WHAT WAS NOT weird in the heat of the moment is very much weird in the light of day.

I feel Alex get up from the bed. I could pretend to be asleep and miss all of this awkwardness, but we're going to have to go through it at some point. And last night, our connection, the heat, the way he wanted me the way I've always wanted him—I can't pretend that wasn't real.

"Hey," I say, my morning voice still a bit ragged.

Alex straightens his back and pulls up his sweatpants before glancing over his shoulder. His smile seems delayed. He swallows hard.

"Hi. I didn't mean to wake you," he says in a hushed tone. He leans over the bed, lifts my head and presses a kiss to the top, in the middle of my messy nest of hair. It's chaste. *Friendly*.

"It's okay. I have to work on a project in the sound lab before your game, so I need to be up too." I slip from my covers. Alex turns back around, apparently to give me privacy.

My turn to swallow hard. I guess we're not so bold during the day. I snag my T-shirt from the floor and slip it over my head, then work my fingers through my hair.

"I was thinking I should get in early, take extra rounds in the cages. You know, impress Coach?" His eye contact with me is minimal, and it makes my chest burn.

"Oh, yeah. That's . . . yeah. Good idea." I turn to find something to busy myself with on my dresser. I settle on my hair band and tilt my head to one side as I gather up my hair to tie it atop my head. Alex is completely dressed, wallet and keys in hand, by the time I face him again.

"You'll be there, yeah?" He chews at his bottom lip.

"Of course," I say, stopping myself mid-step toward him. My shoulders drop, and I look to at my floor.

"Hey, no," Alex says, closing the distance between us.

He tips my chin up and meets my gaze. My eyes are teary and I'm embarrassed by it, but fuck, man! How can I not feel terrified right now? I wrap my hands around his wrists and he cradles my face and runs his thumbs across my damp cheeks. I sniffle. Stupid emotions.

"We'll talk about this when I'm not running off to a game. Give it the attention it deserves. Do it right." He drops his chin a touch and levels me with his serious face. This is the way he looked at me when we were kids and I was afraid of something. He'd pull me aside and talk away my fears. I hope he can do that now. Still.

I know I should wait for when we have the time, but my gut won't let me keep my mouth shut.

"Do you regret it?"

His eyes flinch—only for a heartbeat, but it happens. I feel it sit heavy in my gut. But before I can call it out, he leans in and presses his lips to mine, the kiss soft, chaste, but very much tender.

"Never," he says, then heads out with his duffle bag and my heart.

I HAVE an hour to kill before Alex's game. I don't want to get there too early and be forced to spend more time with Alicia than necessary. If she even shows up again.

There is a tiny smug part of me that hopes she'll see me and just know—that glow about me, is that a thing? But I'm still twisted about how abruptly he left. And I wonder if he would have said anything at all if I hadn't caught him.

Shaking my morning off, I bury myself in the sound lab and my project for my film and sound class. I've been recasting a soundtrack over a classic movie, changing the feel of specific scenes and turning the story into something else entirely. It's a pretty cool assignment, but for some reason the gothic moodiness I've been trying to get just right isn't translating at all.

I slip my headphones down and scan the lab for our student assistant.

"Hey, Chris? Can you give this a listen and tell me what I'm doing wrong?"

"Sure," he says, practically skipping over. He's a grad student in his thirties, and I truly have never met a person who loves their job more. He's also really good. Especially on film work.

He rolls a spare chair over and unplugs my headphones, scanning the visuals on my sound then dragging the player back to the beginning of this section. He presses play then sits back, holding his chin with his palm as he studies the screen.

"Do you mean to have that constant tone in there?" He leans forward and turns down some of the midrange dials on my mixer.

"I . . . I'm not sure." I actually didn't hear them.

I watch the screen as he drags the player back and replays the section we just heard. It sounds exactly the same to me.

"There, yeah. I think you've got it. Pretty cool, Nikki!" He gets up from his chair and I smile and mutter, "Thanks."

My gaze flashes back to the screen, and I twist the dials like I had them before, then lower them again. I shake my head, confused as to why I'm not hearing the same thing Chris seemed to. I pull my headphones back on and run through the same fifteen seconds over and over, never once hearing the difference.

An uneasiness takes over, and I'm not sure if my ears are ringing because of stress or because of the onslaught of decibels. I'm usually pretty careful when I work. I've never been one to blast my music in my ear, and I'm not a fan of the thumping in the car. Too much bass washes out the good stuff. But I did hit a lot of live shows last month, and I do gravitate toward the stages—and the speakers. Maybe I just need to give my ears a rest. I bet that's why I had that bout of vertigo.

I pack up my workstation and take my backpack to my room to drop it off before Alex's game. He hasn't brought up the party tonight, the one Brayden mentioned, so I'm not sure whether he's going to want to go or if he'd rather spend time alone. There's a lot up in the air about us, and it was good that he acknowledged we need to talk about what happened. But shouldn't it be *easy* to talk about?

"Gah! Stop obsessing, Nikki!" I scold myself. I switch out my sweatshirt for my usual black hoodie then slip back into my lucky Alex jersey. I managed to rinse out the smudges from his eye black. I'm smirking to myself when a light knock at my door pushes it the rest of the way open. For a second, my heart leaps at the thought that it's Alex somehow. Minutes before his game. Rushed over here to kiss me and say he loves me.

"Hey, Nik. Seats for three today?" Omar says.

I shake off my crazy thoughts and try to hide my embarrassed laugh, turning to the side and focusing on the buttons of Alex's jersey.

"Three, huh? Does this mean I finally get to meet your

hottie lacrosse boy—" My mouth hangs open in a giant O as the moment my head snaps up, Omar's, well, we don't know what to call him yet, is standing in the middle of my room with his hand out for a shake.

"Oh, my God." I squeeze my eyes shut and slowly cover my face with my palm.

"Is that what he calls me?" Brian whispers, a hint of humor in his tone.

I spread my fingers to peek through them and nod.

"Yes," I admit.

"Nicole Thomas, you traitor!" Omar shouts from the doorway.

Brian laughs hard while I take his hand. Omar's cheeks turn a cherry red.

"Nice to meet you, *Brian*." I make it a point to clearly say his name.

"And you are Nikki," he says.

I nod.

"It's nice to meet Omar's pushy friend," he says as our hands part.

"Pushy?" I jut my neck forward to catch Omar's eyes.

He shrugs.

"What? You're pushy! And stubborn. And a total hopeless romantic," he adds that last part in with a roll of his eyes.

"Maybe not *entirely* hopeless," I let slip out.

"Oh, now, what is this?" Omar's eyebrows rise about seventy inches—okay, maybe three. My pulse picks up as I mentally replay what happened in this room twelve hours ago. I audibly breathe out, which my friend naturally picks up on and starts to fan himself.

"You've got stories and I need them," he says.

"Me, too. Even though we just met. I need them," Brian adds.

My shoulders shirk up, and I feel the blush creeping up my chest and neck.

"Maybe let me sort it out for myself first? I'm not entirely sure what to make of my last twenty-four hours," I say, giving my friend something but far from everything.

"*Mmm*, okay. Clock is ticking on details though. Now, let's get your ass to the game before that man of your dreams has a meltdown because you aren't there," Omar says.

Brian's eyebrow quirks; he's clearly intrigued.

"He won't have a meltdown," I add as I walk out my door. "He's my best friend, and I don't miss his games."

"She hasn't missed one—ever," Omar adds.

I eye him over Brian's shoulder, and he holds out his palms. Damn him for being right.

"This friend of yours must be special," Brian says, as if he doesn't already know everything Omar has surely told him. The two of them have been "talking," as Omar likes to call it, since the basketball game dare. It's been roughly a week, and I know that new relationships are filled with butterflies and excitement, but there's something truly compatible about these two. I see it in how they walk together, the way Omar elbows him in jest and the way

Brian responds, squeezing Omar's shoulders both playfully and affectionately. They're rather perfect.

God, maybe the two of them can sort out the entirety of my love life without me and then I can just pop back in when everything's fixed.

As is my curse, we get to the stadium and find my seat once again occupied by Alicia. She only has one friend with her today, and not the one I was chatting with. I'm rather relieved, actually, because there won't be any familiarity between me and this other girl.

"So, are we sitting elsewhere?" Omar asks, cupping his mouth as if that somehow turns his voice into a whisper.

"No, I'm a big girl," I say, beelining toward my row. I stop by Alicia's knee.

"Mind?" I gesture to the open row beside her.

She sighs but stands, clutching her phone to her bare midriff as she lets me pass. It's chilly out again, not the weather for a half-cut sweatshirt like she's wearing. I'm not stupid. And I've been the girl who tries to catch Alex's eye more than once. But I'm the one who had him on his knees last night, so as I hoped I would, I pass by her with a smug smile. It lasts until I reach my seat and the thought that he's been on his knees for her sets in.

"You okay? You look ill," Omar says, never missing a beat.

"Oh, yeah. Actually, I need to make an appointment. I've had this ear thing," I say, shifting in my seat to pull out my phone.

I built in a buffer today, moving about four seats down

from Alicia but still in the right area so Alex can spot me. I scan the field for him and catch him warming up with Cole in the outfield.

My mom texted me the insurance information yesterday, so I memorize the number I need to input and open the student health app to make an appointment. I find one open slot for Monday and grab it, hoping they'll be able to get me some drops or an antibiotic and clear up whatever's going on.

I didn't realize before just how much my ears have been ringing, but after Chris sampled my mix and made those changes, I started to pay attention. They haven't stopped ringing since then, and it's been an hour. And I kind of feel it's been this way for weeks.

Satisfied that I'm taking action, I put my phone away and turn my attention to the field. Alex is jogging toward us, picking up his stretching bands from the grass, then his glove. His head bops up and his eyes spot me instantly. He touches the brim of his hat, like a cowboy says hello, but I know that little gesture is for me. And I let it paint a smile on my lips as I sink back into my seat and wait for my man to break out of his slump.

**10 /
alex**

NOTHING BUT WALKS.

That's it. I primed myself to show what I've got today. And walks. Three walks.

Sure, I was on base and I scored three times. Stole third, too. But I walked. And Edwin? He knocked it out of the fucking park.

Nikki is waiting for me outside the clubhouse and I have no idea what to say to her. It was easier to cry in front of her than navigate what I've done to us. *What was that in her room? Why did I leave like that?*

I watched her sleep for hours. She must have been tired because I ran my hand through her hair half the damn night and she didn't move. I was in shock at what we'd done—*what I did to us*. Maybe it's a good thing I got shit pitches today because I was pretty gassed energy-wise. I stole that base on adrenaline and luck, with a nice boost from Brayden who made a point to say his family was coming out today—his *whole* family. I doubt his cousin is here, but still. What a dick!

"Good game today, yo," Edwin says, slapping my shoulder with his batting gloves as he passes on the way to his cubby.

"Hey, good game yourself. Nice knock, man!" I reach toward him with a fist and he pounds it.

Not only is he a beast at the plate but he's fucking really nice guy. And his work ethic is admirable. He told me he looked up to me before the game and that he wants to be a team leader like I am by the time he's a senior. I held it in because I'm a little jaded, but I should have told him, "Kid, you'll be drafted before then."

Maybe I'll luck out and get to play with him at the next level. I'd like that. I think I have things to teach him, but I also think I can learn a lot from him. His discipline at the plate. My dad would like the dude.

Dad.

It sucks that he's not here, but also, he's the last person I want to see. I don't need him in my head. It's too bad we could never separate the coach from the father. I still like the coach part. But what he's done to my mom? Yeah, I hate him for it.

"Hey, there he is!" Brayden's voice booms throughout the clubhouse, and a few heads turn to watch our exchange. I know I've been giving off a cold vibe, and he's been pretty obvious with his opinion of me. But the last week has really escalated. His needling has gotten constant—personal.

"Yeah, here I am. And I'm about to leave," I deadpan, forcing my gaze straight ahead at the hanger my jersey was hung from this morning while I shove my wallet, keys, and phone into my duffel.

"Hey, Alex." He stops right next to me, sitting down and straddling the bench, his stupid arm icing because, yeah, of course, he had a great outing today.

I take a deep breath and pull my lips in tight before turning to face him.

"What?" I don't bother pretense. I keep my eyes right on his. Most people get really uncomfortable with this type of alpha challenge. It's a move my dad has with other coaches and umps, and it's gotten him tossed from plenty of games.

Brayden? He's looking right back at me, unfazed. His lip ticks up and he breathes a short laugh through his nose.

"So, you and Nikki coming to the party tonight?"

Her name hits my chest and I want to wrap it up and protect it. Swallow it. Own it.

I shrug.

"Maybe." I actually forgot about the stupid baseball house party. And I'm not sure I want to define my relationship with Nikki in front of a bunch of drunk athletes looking to get laid. Especially this one.

"Well, I invited her. Hope she'll come." He smirks as he gets to his feet.

My glare drills through his skull as he walks away. Before he leaves, he tosses out, "Nice walks today."

When the clubhouse door shuts I throw my duffel at my cubby so hard I might have cracked my phone inside.

"Fuck him!" I let out, having enough sense to know that the only guys left in here understand where I'm coming from.

Brayden's good. And he's liked because he's good, and he has a house that his parents bought for him and he rents out to share with other players. They basically bought him friends. What the hell Nikki ever saw in him beats me.

I plop down and rest my elbows on my knees so I can rub my temples and stare at the concrete floor.

"You shouldn't let him get to you. You know it's all about Nikki and his fragile ego. Just . . . let it go," Cole says, resting his foot next to me while he finishes pulling the tape from his wrist.

I glance up, my eyes feeling the weight of all these things I don't know how to verbalize; the biggest one is the question burning a hole through my insides—am I going to do something to lose Nikki?

"I know. It's mostly my mental game, and I really wanted to come away from today with hits." That part's true, and it's very much the anchor pulling me down to the depths of frustration.

"The hits will come. They always do." He sounds so much like my dad with that response that I laugh, but for the moment, it works to pull me out of my pity party.

"You going to this thing tonight?" I ask him as we walk out together.

He shrugs, but I know him. He'll be there if the volley-ball team shows up. He's in love with no less than five of the players. And given that Cutter never likes to miss a party and is dating the queen of volleyball, the odds are high.

"Alright, well, I'll see ya, man," I say, and he chuckles as we grasp hands.

"Yeah, you probably will. Hey, Nik," he says with a nod over my shoulder.

A tornado takes over my insides, roaring up my esoph-agus and closing off my lungs. How can I be so excited to see her and so afraid at the same time? I turn around and breathe in, forcing the tight smile that seems to be my go-to today. Omar's with her, and another guy. I wonder if that's the lacrosse player he's been crushing on for weeks.

"Where will we see him?" Nikki asks, her hand planting on my bicep as she steps up on her toes and moves to kiss me.

I give her my cheek. *I give her my fucking cheek!*

The hurt is apparent in her eyes as soon as she flattens to her feet and lets her hand drop back down into her pocket. I've already fucked this up. It's just, we haven't talked about it.

"Party at the baseball house, but I don't know if I'm up for it," I say, looking down the walkway that leads to the parking lot because I can't seem to get myself to look at her. I think I'm actually scared. *Shit, I'm terrified.*

"Right, well. I'm going, so I'll either see you there or I won't," she says.

I know that tone, and it snaps me out of my own shit in time to watch her start to walk away.

"We'll, uh, we're gonna go grab some food. I'll let you two—" Omar brings his shoulders up and flattens his mouth.

"Yeah, sorry. I think maybe I fucked up. I'll fix it," I say.

"You always do," he says, and I think there's a subtle dig in there, which I probably deserve. I'll need to unpack that some other time. Right now, I need to go save the burning embers of my bond with the most important person in my life.

"Sorry, man. I'm . . ." I hold out my hand for Omar's companion.

We shake.

"Brian. Nice to meet you. We can chat more next time," he says, nodding toward the pissed off brunette pounding pavement as fast as she can to get away from me.

"Yeah," I sigh. "Again, sorry."

I nod to them both, then swing my bag over my shoulder as I shift into a jog.

"Nik, wait up!"

Her hands are balled into fists at her sides. This is exactly what I was afraid of! Changing our relationship had these risks.

"Hey, I'm running. Seriously, wait!"

She stops in her tracks, and I catch up to her in

seconds. I step in front of her and glance over her shoulder before looking her in the eyes.

"What, making sure Omar and Brian aren't around to see you talk to me?" She folds her arms over her chest and pops out her hip. Fuck, just like her mom. Like my mom!

I pinch the bridge of my nose and squeeze my eyes shut. I have to be honest with her. That's something that never can go away between us.

"Yeah, shit. I'm sorry, I was. I just—" I lift my chin and meet her eyes, the hurt even more obvious now, thanks to the tears pooling in the corners.

"Dammit," she huffs, running her sleeve over her eyes. Always the tough girl.

"No. That look on your face? That's my fault. And I know it. I'm just struggling."

I shake my head and shrug. Her eyes narrow.

"I asked you," she says.

My stomach tightens, and I know what she means, but I don't answer because I swore I'd be honest here. And I don't want to be honest. The truth is going to sound awful, but I swear it's not.

"You know what I'm talking about, Alex! I asked you if you regretted what we did. And you said no. But is that not the truth? Do you? Do you regret kissing me?" She steps in close and drops her hands.

"Seeing me? All of me?" Her voice is raspy. I did that to her too.

I lick my lips and mine my soul.

"No, Nikki. I do not regret what we did. And if we

went back in time right now, I would do it again. And I wouldn't regret it again."

She chews at her lips that are held together tight.

"But?" she finally lets out.

I swallow.

"But . . . I don't know what's next." There, that's as close as I can get to explaining this churn of uncertainty.

"What do you *want* to be next?"

That question lands in my stomach like a brick. I'm living a dream. Nikki has always been in a box, one I've built and kept tidy and been very careful not to mess up. Now there is no box. And what if that means she disappears?

"How do I be your friend, and also—" I widen my eyes and tilt my head.

"See me naked?" she laughs out.

I huff and turn around, grabbing the back of my neck in frustration.

"Don't make this a joke," I demand as I shuffle my feet until I'm facing her again.

Her expression doesn't read *joke*. Her frown has softened, though. She moves into me, pulling my arm down and skimming her palm down my forearm until she takes my hand in hers and flattens it on the center of her chest.

"I'm not going anywhere," she says. And for the first time since I left her room this morning, my shoulders relax and my stomach pauses its churn.

"No?" I stare deep into her eyes, not a hint of anything but resolve in them.

She shakes her head then slowly inches closer, moving her other hand to the neck of my hoodie as she lifts up on her toes.

I suck in my bottom lip and nod before kissing her, soft and sweet, nothing like the rabid animal I was last night. Her lips are like a gift, and just having her touch me somehow makes things better.

"Now, are you coming to this party with me? Or not?" Her mouth lifts on one side.

I roll my eyes, then swing an arm around her and coax her to walk alongside me, stuck to me like glue.

"Yeah, I guess we can party."

I walk her back to her room, kissing her one more time before promising to be back within the hour to pick her up for dinner at Patty's then a party with the fools on my team. That feeling creeps back into my chest, though, when I'm about halfway home. And I finally pin down the source of everything.

It's not Nikki I'm worried about. It's me. And so far this year my track record for holding the important shit together is zero for two.

**11 /
nikki**

OKAY. So maybe it *is* weird.

And perhaps Alex hasn't spent years thinking about this version of us the way I have.

But we're here now. I guess I'm simply more prepared and know what I want. And as far as I know, my family isn't breaking up while my dream threatens to slip away.

We hold hands in the car, and I expect him to shift us back into *old* Alex and Nikki when we walk through the door of Brayden's house. But instead, he swings his arm around me and pulls me in close, kissing the top of my head.

I blink up at him and he smirks, lifting a shoulder.

"Effort," he says.

"That's all I ask for." *For now*.

I let Alex lead me through what is already a fairly crowded living room. Half of his teammates are piled on the oversized sectional, some sitting on the back, all playing some video game with an obscene amount of graphic blood.

I nudge Alex's side with my elbow and he utters, "Rage issues. All of them, pitchers."

I laugh quietly but stop suddenly when Alex and I literally run into Brayden. His cologne is taking center stage tonight, and I wriggle my nose trying not to sneeze.

"You made it," he says, lifting an arm to hug me. He stops short, though, when he realizes Alex's arm is already there.

"Oh," he says, his eyes blinking rapidly a few times as his brow lifts.

"Yeah, *oh*," Alex says, and I can't help but note the smug tone.

"Alright, well, I'm going to get a drink. And then if it's all right with the host, I'd like to get some tunes going?" I glance between the two of them, neither of them looking down at me and both wearing the same expression, like a mask made of bravado and dares.

"Sure. That'd be great, Nik. You pick the vibe," Brayden says, his mouth spending extra time on that last word.

I roll my eyes at their pissing contest and head into the kitchen, where I find Cole doing his best to entertain a girl who towers over him. Clearly one of Laney's teammates.

"Hey, Nikki can tell you. She was at the game. Nik, tell Aria about my diving catch today." Cole slips behind me then thrusts me forward with his hands on my shoulders.

I sigh but I like Cole, so I'll build him up if he thinks that's what he needs.

"Yeah, it was prettttttty awesome. Saved the game, basically." I tilt my head and shrug on one side to sell it, then immediately turn my attention to the cooler filled with ice and beer.

"Mind grabbing me one?" Brayden says, his chin hovering over my shoulder.

I dig my hand into the ice and lift up a cold bottle, stopping myself from swinging my arm just a little too far and popping him in the nose. His quiet laugh sends his breath snaking over my skin.

He pulls off the cap then touches the chilled side of the glass to my shoulder. I feel it through the cotton of my T-shirt.

"You take this one," he says, shifting to cut off my exit.

My mouth hangs open for a second while I weigh the best words to use, and in that split second, my eyes lock with Alex's from the other room. I swear I can see his pupils dilating, even from several feet away. His jaw is clenched, and his mouth a straight line. Seeing him look so possessive feels good.

"Actually"—I turn into Brayden enough that my elbow pushes into his diaphragm. He takes a tiny step back— "I'm the driver tonight. Gotta make sure our all-star gets home safe, you know?" I reach into the nearby fridge and pull out a water bottle before nodding toward Alex, who is now only a few steps away.

"All-star, huh? Not if you keep up those numbers. Right, Alex?" Brayden takes a long, purposeful sip of his beer as his gaze dims on Alex's face.

"Hey, didn't you two date a while back?" Alex shifts his weight so he's leaning into the counter across from me but his eyes never leave Brayden's face.

"And on that note . . ." I say, rounding the counter and patting Alex on the upper back as I pass.

I weave my way back through the living room to the media center set up in the corner. Because I *did*, in fact, date Brayden for a little while, I'm familiar with his pad. Little has changed over the last couple years, and the computer set-up is basically the same. Unfortunately, so is his music library.

"Ugh," I huff out, logging in to my cloud so I can pull some of my new favorites together and get a house beat going.

"Hey, sorry. I maybe got a little—"

"Alpha?" I lift my brow as I glance up at Alex. He swallows sheepishly.

"Yeah." His voice is meek, which is sort of cute.

"It's fine. But for the record, I don't really want to be weaponized and used in whatever this beef is you have going on with Brayden. And ah!" I hold up my hand before he speaks, and Alex stops with his mouth open. "Before you say that there is no beef, check yourself. There's beef. I smell it. Everyone smells it. And you, Alex Mendoza, are going to explain it to me later."

I give him a tightlipped grin as he breathes in slowly through his nose and eventually nods.

"I am," he says.

"Hey, A! You loan me some cash? We're getting a game going," Cole hollers from the kitchen.

Alex's eyes flutter closed and I laugh, then pat him in the center of the chest. He could pay his tuition off of the amount of money he's *loaned* Cole over the years.

"Yeah, I'll spot you. Deal me in too." He shakes his head as he opens his eyes to mine.

"Go have fun. I'm in my happy place," I say, pressing play without looking to kick off one of my new audio discoveries. Her name is Eloki, and her sound has this way of transporting me into an underground speakeasy where girls smoke foot-long cigarettes and men walk around with Zippo lighters. She's smooth and unique. Brilliant.

"This is good," Alex says, pointing up as he leans in for a kiss. I smirk, unable to stop my mind from recalling him saying those very same words in this same exact room three years ago.

"I know," I say, closing the gap between us to peck his lips.

I catch a few eyes on us as he walks away, a couple of girls whispering in the corner then immediately taking to their phones to investigate or spread the gossip. Rather than dwell on their opinions, I lose myself in my passion, moving from song to song and garnering a small audience of my own.

Two hours pass in a blink. I'm a little lightheaded,

partly from the blue screen light, I'm sure, but I also think I might be a tad dehydrated. I didn't drink much at the game, and the wind tends to suck the moisture out of all living things.

The stakes in the poker game must be getting pretty serious because at least half the party is gathered around the card table in the dim kitchen. I push my way through the crowd to get to the fridge and grab a cold bottle of water. I knock about half of it back before leaning my elbows on the counter to join the others in watching the intense showdown happening between Alex and the rest of the table. His tongue pushed against the inside of his cheek, his smile is off-center and hard to discern. His drunken eyes are heavy, and his blinking is slow. I'm the only one in this room who knows he's bluffing. I'm sure of it. As good as he is at masking his emotions, I can see the cracks. He's had three, maybe four beers since he sat down to play. And the man can hold a lot more.

This look? It's calculated.

"Well? You calling or what?" he says, lifting a brow as he flattens his cards face down on the table and takes a long swig from his beer. His eyes reach me mid-drink, and I tilt my head slightly, hazing my eyes with suspicion. His body shakes with the smallest laugh. He knows I've caught him.

"Where's my lucky charm?" he calls, stretching his arm out toward me then waving me in.

"I'm comfy right here," I say, a little in protest.

What started as pretend flirting and vague shows of

affection seems to have gotten the intended results. Brayden is definitely paying a lot more attention to me. And when his focus isn't on me, I feel like it's somehow tethered to me. Like right now, as he stares hard at Alex's face from the other side of the table. Sure, this is a poker duel. But also, is it for the girl? Is this a gunfight at dawn?

"Aww, come on, Nik. I need you to tell me what you think about my cards." Alex's eyes lock on mine, and I see right through the haze into him. Something is different tonight.

"Fine," I huff, capping my water and bringing it with me to stand behind him. I begin to hunch down, but Alex turns to the side, offering me his lap instead. My heart thumps once and only once, loud and heavy.

"Okay," I say in a nervous whisper. His hand slides around my bare midriff until his thumb hooks through the belt loop on my jeans.

This is not the first time I've sat on Alex's lap. There were plenty of times I had to get a boost to see a movie or share a seat in his dad's pickup truck when he unsafely buckled both of us in one seat. And in high school, there was the time we had to smash balloons on each other's laps for class wars. I blushed then. But now? I'm on fucking fire.

Alex tilts his hand up enough for me to get a glimpse of his bullshit cards. I don't flinch, and I'm careful not to blink too fast or too slow. But I do utter, "I knew it," then turn to match his smirk.

"Knew what?" Brayden asks.

I start to glance in Brayden's direction but Alex's fingertips coax my chin to remain right where it is. I lick my lips and his eyes flicker to my mouth for a beat.

I'm not sure whether this is part of Alex's act or if he's truly this into me right now. But in this room where these guys, in particular, are constantly comparing their dick sizes, he's declaring himself the winner. And I dare say, judging from the hard-on pressing into my ass right now, I'm apt to crown him king.

"Fine. I fold," Brayden says, tossing his cards to the center of the table atop a pile of fives and tens. Alex's mouth curls and I shake my head in warning. He might not be drunk but he's too buzzed to listen to reason, and he flips his cards over to show off the fact that Brayden just threw away what I quickly estimate to be about seventy-five dollars.

"Fuck you, Mendoza!" Brayden shouts, surging to his feet and shoving the table forward hard enough that it pushes me from Alex's lap and onto the floor.

"Watch yourself," Alex says, his voice surprisingly calm as he kicks his chair back and lunges to offer me his hand.

His eyes are steely, and his expression seems guarded. His bluffing has not ended.

"You okay?" he asks, his hand gentle along my cheek.

I nod but my eyes shift to where Brayden is rushing him. I open my mouth to warn him, but it comes out too late as he slams his foot into the center of Alex's back, shoving him into me.

"That's enough of this," he says.

I grasp at his arm to no avail in an attempt to stop him. Within seconds, he's back on his feet, his entire body bulldozing Brayden backward until he stumbles on his feet and falls through the screened door that leads to the back patio. The second Brayden gets back up, Alex assails him with a fist to the jaw, the crack loud enough that you can hear it inside over my music, which someone pauses. I blink, and in that time, the entire party is gathered while Alex paces around Brayden in a half circle.

"Ha, you're a joke," Brayden says, getting up on one knee. He spits blood onto the concrete, then wipes the cut on his lip with his sleeve.

Alex points at him, his head shaking and jaw clenched.

"You're the joke," he growls.

"Alex. Come on," I say as I get to the open door frame, bits of torn screen flapping in the breeze. Embers pop from the firepit nearby, and a light stream of traffic hums from the highway in the distance. For a college party, it's suddenly eerily silent.

Alex's gaze shifts to me, his head falling to the side. *I'm sorry*, he mouths.

It's okay, I mouth back. But in many ways, it's not. Maybe adding an *us* on top of the stress he's dealing with is too much. I shouldn't have let our relationship change so fast.

I take his hand, though, because that change has come and gone. It's accelerated. One fist to my ex's jaw propelled the story of Alex and Nikki several chapters ahead. And I need Alex to know that even after this, I'm keeping him. We aren't going back, not that we even could if we wanted to. And I'm not going anywhere, like I just said.

"You know what, Mendoza? You can keep her," Brayden says just as we're about to cross the threshold back into the house. My eyes close as I will him to just stop there. I can handle him spitting out insults if that's what he needs to do to save face. He won't hurt me, and I'm pretty sure the people in this house will see him a whole lot differently now anyhow.

But Alex? I'm not so sure he'll be able to handle the insults. There are a few things he's always defended with every ounce of fight in his body—my honor, and his mom's. And that was before, when we were just friends.

"Hey, maybe I'll call up your mom instead," Brayden says, the drunken slur taking over. Or perhaps he's just been punched drunk.

Alex stops with one foot in the door. I grip his arm and flatten my palm to his bicep, willing him to look me in the eyes. He does, and I can tell that all it would take is for me to give him permission. I won't. Because his scholarship is on the line and he's pushed it enough as is tonight. The last thing he needs is to seriously hurt Brayden to the point of an ER visit.

"Yeah, I hear she's single now. Your dad shacking up with a student probably left her good and lonely. I bet she could use some lovin'," Brayden laughs out.

I manage to squeeze Alex's arm tight enough to force him to remain grounded, at least for a half second. In that time, I spin around, march up to Brayden's bloodied face, and smack it with my open palm so hard that his head flails to one side.

"Shame on you," I spit out, turning back around and marching through the silent party with my best friend's hand clutched in mine.

**12 /
alex**

NIKKI PULLS UP to the curb in front of my rental house and kills the engine. The street is dark and quiet since most of the people who live off campus are either in bed or at Brayden's party.

"Fucking Brayden."

She breathes out a short laugh. She's been vibrating with anger for minutes. The drive home was quiet. She didn't even bother to turn music on. *Very* unlike Nikki.

"I'm sorry he treated you that way," I say, unclicking the safety belt and letting it zip across my chest.

"You're sorry about Brayden," she says, not quite the same thing I said. Noticeably different, in fact.

I turn and find her eyes narrowed on me, her elbow resting on my steering wheel.

"'Just the distraction you need,' you said."

I inhale through my nose and sink into the corner so I can look her in the eyes.

"I said that, yeah. But that was before—" Before I was willing to break my own rules.

"Alex, were you using me to get back at Brayden?" She doesn't blink. She simply stares at my eyes and waits for the read. Just like back at the house when she knew I was bluffing at that table, she knows the truth right now.

"I was." It's better to own it.

"Fucking damn, Alex!"

She gets out of the car, slams the door, and stomps down the middle of the street with her hands threaded behind her head. I wait a few seconds until she stops, then get out and move to the front of my car to sit on the hood.

Her head falls back, her eyes on the stars. I'm sure she's stringing together a few swear words, maybe even mixing English with Spanish the way her mom does. The way *my* mom does. Seems I'm always making the women in my life do that.

She turns eventually, taking her time to walk back to me, stopping out of arm's reach.

Her head tilts to the side.

"Why does he know so much about your dad?"

I chuckle, but it's not a happy one.

"Guess who Miss Arendale's first cousin is?"

Understanding hits her, at least I think. Her weight eases back as her lips part, and she hums, "*Oh.*"

I push up from the car, relieved when she doesn't take a step back. She eyes me skeptically.

"You wanna come in?" I want her to come in. I'm still

angry, but also, I'm still thinking about the way she felt sitting on my lap, the way her bare stomach felt when my hand slid across it. The way she smells and tastes. All of the pieces of her I have yet to explore.

"Yeah. I'll come in," she says, and I move closer, reaching for her hand. She crosses her arms quickly, though, sneering at me.

"You have to earn my hand," she says, jokingly. But also . . . there's some truth there.

We don't get to spend nights here often, and she'll have to go back to her dorm by morning. But it's rare to have the house empty. I should probably sober up a little and then spend tonight talking—*really* talking. The last thing I want to do right now, though, is talk.

I lock the door behind us then flip on the small hall light that shines on up the stairs. She leads the way and I trail behind her, trying not to be a total pervert staring at her ass. That's no different from before, however. Even when we were friend-zoned, I stared at her ass.

"Your room is actually clean," she notes, kicking the only discarded piece of clothing on my floor up in the air and snagging it. It's my favorite hoodie. It's also *her* favorite hoodie, and she hugs it to her chest and drops her chin, pressing her nose into the fabric.

"It probably needs a wash," I say.

She shakes her head.

"It smells like you." Her gaze holds on to me as I move across the room and sit on the edge of my bed.

"You wanna kick my ass in Xbox or something?"

That's what we would have done if this conversation were happening a week ago.

She shakes her head. I bite my bottom lip, strangely nervous about how to go about this.

"I'm really sorry, Nik. About . . . about using you to get at Brayden like that. It wasn't right."

She inhales and sucks her mouth into a straight line before nodding.

I glance down at the floor, my muscles still twitching a little from throwing punches and shoving Brayden through a screen door. *Fuck, I'm going to feel really embarrassed about that later.*

I lick my lips, then bite the tip of my tongue before glancing up at her through my lashes. Her gaze was waiting for me.

"It wasn't *all* about making him jealous."

"No?" she whispers.

I shake my head.

"There was a part of me that really liked the excuse to see what it was like," I admit.

She smirks, then turns to the side and tosses my sweatshirt on top of my desk. She steps closer, and when I reach out this time, she willingly gives me her fingertips, balancing them individually, meticulously, on each of mine.

"And what was it like?" She quirks a brow.

A low laugh rumbles in my chest.

"The flirting bit? Holding your hand and maybe, touching you, like . . . right . . . here?" I brush the back of my hand across her bare stomach. She quivers. "That was a pretty great hall pass."

"Hall pass, huh?" She kicks one of her feet forward, tapping her toe against mine.

"Yeah, it was a hall pass. I knew it was temporary." It was supposed to be temporary. But then I felt her. Not just her body but the way she cares about me. I felt it all at once. And I kissed her. *Everywhere*. And we can't go back.

"We're way past temporary, Alex."

"I know," I agree.

My tongue pushes in the side of my cheek, my gaze fixed on the very hard peaks of her tits poking through her white cotton crop top. My eyes flit up quickly to hers.

"I know we need to talk. But I'm still pretty wound up from what happened," I admit.

"Me too."

I move my hands to the bottom of her shirt and gather up two fistfuls, bringing the material up her body until it stops right at the edge, showing off just enough skin. How did I not know she wasn't wearing a bra all night?

My gaze moves back to her face.

"I know we're friends, Nikki. But I want to fuck like we're enemies."

Neither of us blinks, but over the next several seconds Nikki draws in a slow deep breath that pushes her chest forward. I tug where I'm grasping her shirt and her breath hitches. She lifts her chin but holds my gaze. It's a stand-off, and the longer it lasts, the harder I get.

I tug again, but she resists, shaking her head slowly and *tsking*.

"This isn't about Brayden," she says. It's not really a question, but she requires my guarantee. I understand. I owe her that.

"Not even remotely close," I say, tugging again.

This time, she obeys, moving into me until her knees hit the edge of the bed. I push her shirt up over her bare tits, rubbing my thumbs over her nipples then pinching the skin, tight. Nikki moves her hand into my hair, pulling my head toward her, coaxing my very willing mouth to suck on her.

I meet her request, covering her tit with my mouth as one hand sweeps behind her back and pulls her into me, hard. My tongue swirls the hard tip while my other hand rolls the opposite peak until they feel like pebbles to the touch.

I hold her nipple hostage in my teeth as I push her shirt up more, urging her to take it off. She tosses it to the floor before her hands move to my back and claw until my shirt is on the floor next to hers.

Her small frame makes it easy to sweep one hand under her ass as her legs wrap around me until she's sitting on my lap, straddling me. I kiss my way from her breast up her neck until my mouth locks on hers. It's not a tender kiss this time. It's possessive. And maybe there is a little bit of me proving something to Brayden in this act. I hate that he ever saw this. Nikki wouldn't say, but he did. He said it *a lot*. I hated it then, and I hate it more now. But this is not just him I'm proving something to. It's all men. Every male that looks at her and thinks they can. That they deserve her time. That they're worthy.

They do not. They *are* not.

Neither am I, but I'm taking what's mine anyway. If our friendship dies because of this, I need to know it was worth it. That I had something so great, so rare and beautiful, in my hands and devoured it. Lived it. Breathed it.

That I spoiled her for everyone else.

I stand up, holding her to me and walking her toward my door until her back is flat against it. Pinned between my body and the wood, I reach down and unzip her jeans, letting her legs down so she can kick off her shoes and strip them away completely. I tug her panties off too, then run my fingers through her soaking wet pussy. Her head hits the door as she moans, her nails digging into my bare shoulders.

"You like to be touched there by me. Don't you?" I want to know how many times she fantasized about this. If she ever touched herself and pretended it was me.

"Yes," she whimpers as my fingers glide along her wet skin then dip inside her. I push two in, not taking my time, and I finger fuck her hard against my door loving the way her eyes glaze over as she stares at me and her mouth hangs open, unable to form words.

I feel her clench around me so I pull out and drop to my knees to taste her. My hands claw at her ass, moving her feet forward enough to give me the angle to drive my tongue inside until she's literally riding my face.

I flick her clit with the tip of my tongue and she pulses, her breath stopping with a sharp cry, so I stop.

"No. Not like that tonight. That's for friends. My cock? That's for enemies," I say, standing and unzipping my jeans to pull my dick free. I wrap my hand around it while Nikki pushes my pants down my hips until they pool at my feet. I kick them, along with my shoes, away, and then I step into her until my hard shaft is pressed up against her belly.

"Do you feel that?" My hand is at her jaw, my thumb on her artery, her pulse beating wildly.

Nikki drags her hands up above her head on her own then glances up, inviting me. I move my hand from her jaw to her wrists. She drops her chin again and our eyes meet.

"Fuck. Me."

I feel myself swell between us at her words. So forceful. So dominant. No mistaking what she wants. Where her line is. There is no line.

I glance to my dresser where my condoms are, then meet her eyes. I know I should, but I don't want to. I want to feel all of her.

She nods her head.

"I'm on the pill," she says.

And that's all I need to unleash the animal trying to completely take over my body. Fisting my cock, I move back a step and lower myself just enough to guide my tip into her wet center. I pull out then slide my cock through her wet pussy a few times before guiding it back in, and this time I drive into her.

"Ahh," she gasps, and I relax my hips then pump into her again.

"Fucking so tight, Nik. You feel so fucking good," I say, rocking back then into her again.

I grab her wrists with both hands, the fact she's so helpless like this and willing to let me have her however I want making me harder. My body rocks into hers, my hips moving up so I can reach her very limit. She brings one leg up, hooking it around my waist, and I step in with more force so she can completely choke my middle with her legs.

"That's my girl," I say, my rhythm picking up while I fuck her against my bedroom door.

My mouth covers her, muffling her cries while I pummel her tight pussy, stretching her, feeding her, making her take all of me. Her hips push into me with every pump, meeting me at every stroke. I let go of her hands and she leaves them up, showing me exactly how bad she likes to be.

Fuck me if any other guy has had her like this. I'll make her forget if they have.

My tongue trails down her jaw and my teeth stop at her bottom lip, tugging it into my mouth and sucking while we shake the wall with our force. My hands cover her tits, my thumb rubbing raw circles around her pebbled nipples, then pinching them when her thighs clench even more around me.

"Do not stop fucking me, Alex. Never. Stop. Never. Stop. Nev—" Her words fall into whimpers as her body clenches around me, her legs squeezing me tight and her hands dropping to my shoulders so she can hold on through her orgasm.

I pump into her, feeling every wave, gritting my teeth to hold out just long enough so she doesn't miss anything she's owed. This will be the best she's ever had. I swear it. I'll make sure of it. If we fail after this, she will never forget the way her pussy feels with my cock inside. So full.

Her body collapses into me, and I hold her right leg up so I can drive into her a few more times until I come inside of her.

"Ahhhh," she moans as I lean into her, my spent body covered in sweat and sticking to hers against my door.

I pull out and take a few slow steps back as she languishes, her shoulder blades resting against the door.

"Spread your legs," I say as her gaze hits mine, her eyes still very much in a trance. She does as I ask.

I take her form in, her perfect breasts, which she squeezes as my gaze rakes over them.

"We'll fucking go again, Nikki," I say, and it's a promise.

Her hand trails down the center of her chest, down her stomach, and over the thin trail of hair until she touches herself. I lick my lips, seeing exactly what I fantasized about. My cum dripping from her, soaking her fingers as she rubs it over her still swollen pussy.

"Suck it," I say, and she drags her fingertips back up

her body, drawing a line of our pleasure up and over her tit, being sure to coat her nipple in it before holding out two fingers and pushing them between her lips.

She tastes us. And it's the fucking hottest thing I've ever seen.

"Let's go again," I say, and she raises her hands back up the door.

13 /
nikki

I KNEW we would be like this physically. At least, I knew *I* would be like this with Alex. I trust him with my life. He may piss me off sometimes, but he would also walk through fire to protect me. And he would never hurt me.

I have never been so open before, so uninhibited. There was my first time, in high school, which I only admitted to Alex because he teased me about being a virgin. It was awful. The guy, our quarterback at the time, was a complete loser, too. He ended up getting an extreme DUI on his way to prom a week after we slept together. He was supposed to meet me there. Thankfully Alex was going with a group of friends, so we ended up *sort of* going together.

My mom obsesses over those photos still. If I weren't mortified at telling her what's transpired, she would probably throw a party and burn incense to somehow woo Alex into proposing. That's always been her dream. Both of our moms', actually. They've been photographing us as if we were a couple since we were babies.

I hope we make it. For them.

For me.

I wasn't worried before. But with everything Alex is going through, I can't help but fear that I really *am* simply a distraction. We need to carve out space for a friend session simply because that seems to be how we are most honest. As friends. And I need more reassurance than I thought I did. I'm not backing out now, but if Alex does, I'm not so sure I can go back to looking at him as simply the boy who sometimes gives me a ride home.

I broke the rules for my job, too. Technically, at least. I snuck in at six in the morning Sunday, and at least one girl on my floor saw me. And she knew. *Oh, she knew.*

I have a head of hair that tells no lies. When I'm confident, it rocks. When I'm sick, it looks lifeless. And when I've spent the night doing really naughty things with the guy I've imagined doing them with for years, well, my hair told the story.

An hour-long shower and a six-hour nap put me back together, and the rest of the day was spent catching up on assignments. I sent my movie score in early, accepting that Chris, our teacher's assistant, wouldn't lead me astray. I'm sure it sounds right if he says so. And the fact I can't tell for sure is why I'm here.

"Nicole Thomas?" A young physician assistant peeks her head out from behind the student health waiting room door. I gather up my backpack and the clipboard with my paperwork.

"Here," I say, rushing over to her.

I hand over my paperwork as she ushers me to the scale. I step on backward, a trick my mom taught me so I don't have to see the number. Numbers demand to be thought about and I'm happy with my body not knowing what number goes along with it. I hush the PA before she can tell me the result.

"I'm going to get some of your vitals really quick. Relax your arm," she says, hooking me up to take my blood pressure. That number, I'm all right knowing. Maybe because it's normal.

"You're here for an ear issue and headaches, is that right?" she says as she enters some of my stats into her computer.

"*Mmm hmm.* And I think maybe my hearing has been off."

She glances up at me but keeps typing.

"Okay. We'll take a look. Dr. Davis will be in shortly."

She tucks my folder in the basket on the door then leaves me alone in the tiny, sterile room. I swing my legs back and forth as I lean back on my palms, the paper sheet crinkling under my weight. I'm not good at waiting in places like this. My mind travels down its own path of worries. I don't even need the help of Google or WebMD to spiral. And I did a little looking on my own as it is, so those initial diagnoses are lodged in my head.

My body starts to warm, so I sit up straight and pull off

my sweatshirt so I can pull the bottom of my T-shirt away from my body to fan myself. The fact I can feel my pulse in my right ear only helps eliminate some of my hypotheses while strengthening others. And when I hear the rapid knock on the door, I jump where I sit and clutch my chest.

"Sorry. There's really no easy way to surprise people like this," the doctor says.

I titter nervously.

"It's all right," I say.

She flips through my paperwork as she smiles, then slides over a stool so she can sit at the computer and review her assistant's notes. She's older, and somehow that puts me at ease—both that she's a woman and that she's hopefully seen whatever I have happening.

"When did the headaches and dizziness start?" She gets to her feet and moves to stand to my right.

"A week. Though, now that I think back, I have had a few over the last couple of months. They come and go."

She presses her scope into my right ear and it warms, from the light I presume.

"Okay," she says. *Is that a good okay? An interesting okay?*

She moves to my left and does the same. The scope feels hotter against my skin, but I think that's simply my nerves.

"And you mentioned that you're having some hearing issues. Have you had a hearing test done?" She still has the scope in my ear as she leans forward to look me in the eyes.

"No." I'm afraid to move my head.

"We can do one here. No problem." She pulls the scope out and moves back to her computer. A few seconds later her assistant pokes her head in.

"Can you bring in the audiometer?" Dr. Davis asks.

Her assistant nods and disappears back through the door. I feel like my world hit fast forward suddenly, my head swiveling as I try to keep up with the doctor's questions and now the equipment being set up in front of the chair. I move to the seat and put on the headphones, which are somehow nicer than mine. The assistant to my right and the doctor on my left, they run me through a series of tones, asking me to raise my corresponding hand when I hear something. It feels like a trick at times because they ask me where the sound is and I hear nothing, so I don't raise a hand.

My worry ramps up when her assistant wheels the system away and Dr. Davis scoots on her stool so we're sitting face-to-face.

"You have a slight infection, which is probably from your own investigations into your ear," she says in a kind way.

I nod because yeah, I went at both ears pretty good with the Q-tips. They did zero good, and apparently a lot of harm. My pulse slows because an infection is what I hoped for. Some antibiotics, drops likely. Maybe another hearing test.

"Nikki, you might also have a small acoustic neuroma in your left ear. That's probably what's causing the dizziness, and I would almost guarantee that's why you have trouble hearing midrange tones."

"I'm sorry, I . . . I'm what?"

I'm going to faint.

"Let me show you," she says, holding up a finger. She swivels the computer table so I can see the screen and the results from the audiometer. I'm not really hearing her, maybe because of the neuroma in my ear or maybe because I'm in a full-blown panic attack, but I'm able to somehow hold it together enough to visually understand the results. The red dots are all sounds I missed. Sounds like the ones I couldn't tune on my project. Like songs I've had trouble with lately on the mixer.

"I'm sorry, but . . . I'm really hot," I say. I lean my weight onto the right arm of the chair while the doctor pushes the computer out of the way so she can fill a cup with water.

"It's natural. It's a lot of medical jargon. I'm sorry," she says, handing me the cup. I take it with two hands, like a toddler. I bring it to my lips slowly and take small sips, focusing on my breathing. I haven't freaked out like this since we were in a minor car accident on our way home from the Iowa State football game when I was twelve.

I'm not sure when her assistant came back in, but I'm grateful for the cool pack she's put on my neck. And my pulse seems to be regulating.

"It isn't serious, and it is common, though not usually in women your age," Dr. Davis continues.

"Okay. What does that mean? For me, I mean. Are you

saying it's not cancer?" This was my biggest fear. Stupid Google.

She shakes her head.

"It's a small noncancerous tumor. The usual course is to monitor it and make sure it doesn't change or grow. And if the vertigo gets worse, we can find ways to treat that, help with the symptoms."

"And the inability to hear midrange tones?" This. This is what I care about most. I would be fine falling over every other day if it meant I could hear everything as it should be.

She pulls her mouth into a tight line, and my chest collapses. I will not cry. Not here.

"There's surgery. It's an option, but I wouldn't recommend it with how small yours likely is. Surgery itself comes with risks, and—"

"I'm a sound engineer," I blurt out.

She stops being a doctor then and there. Her expression softens, her eyes rounding. She looks down at her hands and nods.

"Before you do anything, you'll need to set up a CT with contrast to confirm the diagnosis. They'll be able to see the size and exactly where it's located. We don't have that here, but the main hospital does. I'll print your referral. You'll want to fast beforehand so I recommend scheduling it in the morning. I'll also print you some information on options for surgery. There's radiation, but . . ."

Her doctor persona is back. She moves her stool back

to the monitor and types feverishly, the small printer whirling to life as it spits out page after page. She gathers them into a hefty stack and steps next to me so she can explain everything I'm going to obsess over for the next however many hours.

Surgery.

Risky.

Only improves hearing fifty percent of the time.

Minutes later, I drag my feet along the walkway from student health toward my dorm. I'm not going to accounting today. Oh, and my dream just blew up in my face.

14 /
alex

MUST BE NICE BEING A PITCHER.

I wondered how Brayden was going to handle logging the study hall hours he's short on for the month. Tiff has really cracked down on academics thanks to the goddamn basketball team's fake grades scandal last year, but based on the database, it looks like *someone* took care of it for him.

Probably one of the grad student coaches. They can get in here without leaving a record, and Coach wouldn't want to get his hands dirty. I don't put it past him to insinuate that someone else should, though, as long as there's no straight line to his office.

I clock in for my time and hover over Brayden's name for a second, entertaining for a second the fantasy of just hitting delete. I don't, though. And I won't say anything because that would be petty; it's for the good of the team that we keep Brayden eligible. His grades are fine. It's study hall.

Honestly, it's also probably good for me that he's not here to show his face because I'm still not sure I'm ready to handle seeing it. I hope that lip of his is fat as fuck.

I drag my backpack to my usual table and flop it in the center. I didn't bring my laptop today and I'm caught up on my reading. I literally have nothing to do, but I have to sit in here anyway and pass two hours of study time because some basketball player couldn't pass general math.

This idle time is bad for me. My mom left me a message this morning and I haven't been able to call her back yet. She's filing for divorce—officially. Well, they *both* are, but it's her decision. Everything gets to be her decision as far as I'm concerned.

When I pull my phone out to shoot my mom a text I see one I've missed from Nikki.

> NIKKI: I'm not feeling great, won't make study hall. Sorry.

I'm more let down than usual that she's not coming, and I feel selfish for it, especially since she's sick. I find I'm anxious to get back to her when I'm away. Not that I haven't always enjoyed every second I spend with her, but there's this tether between us now. I feel like she's starting to breathe for me, and without her, my lungs never seem quite as full.

> ME: It's OK. I don't have anything to do so I'm sure I would drive you nuts. I'll come by as soon as my time is up.

I think about adding a heart but hit send without one instead. It would be sweet, but hearts are not really our thing. At least, I don't *think* it's our thing. One more agenda item I need to mentally add to our much overdue talk.

I'm about to open my sports app so at least I can stream a game while I'm in here when she texts me back.

NIKKI: It's all right. I'm probably just going to sleep. I'll call you if I wake up before dinner.

Okay. Now, I'm worried.

I flatten the phone on the table and scan the study hall space. It's filling up, and it's one of the track coaches sitting in the office today, monitoring poorly with his back to the door. I'm cool with those guys anyhow, and they don't give two shits about the school's policy since they're track and always get the short end of the stick in sports funding. I move my bag from the table and set it on the floor next to my right leg, leaving the strap in my hand while I wait for the perfect moment.

I spot Cole after a few seconds and nod as he checks in. I get to my feet as he walks over, but wait at my seat. He stops next to me and his brow draws in when he spots my bag dangling from my hand.

"Don't be stupid," he says under his breath as his eyes flit back to my face.

My head tilts to the side as I sigh.

"I'm not. I logged in already and it's the track guys. Nikki's sick, and I—"

Cole smirks.

"Don't fucking start," I warn him, but there's a small part of me that also likes how right he has been all along.

"I'm not starting anything. Just, it's sweet that you want to risk ineligibility so you can take your girlfriend soup. That's all." His lips pucker like one of those gossipy women that go get their hair done with my mom. She used to take me with her when I was little, and the stories they told probably gave me more sex education than the actual course taught at our high school.

"Just, sit in my seat, would you? So it looks like you were always here. I guarantee they aren't watching that closely." I slide my chair back a few more inches and nudge him to hurry.

"Yeah, yeah. I got your back," Cole says, taking my seat and dropping his own backpack at his feet. He glances up at me with the smile of a six-year-old.

"What?" I ask, checking the office door one more time. It's open but the coach inside is still sitting with his feet up and his back to the room.

"Are you going to scoot my chair in like a gentleman?" His lips quirk into this tight fucking smug expression as he barely contains his laugh.

"You're an ass, Cole. Get to work," I say, leaving him to snicker quietly like Cookie Monster behind me.

I slip back out the door without a sound and, luckily, don't run into anyone else from the team on my way out.

I go the long way just to be safe, circling the media center and walking along the street to avoid the sports offices on my way to the campus café. Cole's soup idea was a good one, so I stop and pick up chicken tortilla along with a bag of Fritos and peanut butter M&Ms, Nikki's favorite. Five minutes later, I'm at her door. I sent her a quick text in case she really is sleeping. I don't want to scare her.

ME: Knock knock

I hold my breath while the message delivers, and I'm relieved when the reply dots pop up.

NIKKI: Who's there?

She adds the eye-rolling emoji and I chuckle loud enough from outside her door she has to hear me. I respond just in case.

ME: Alex

Her door opens about a second later and her eyes widen with surprise.

"What are you doing here?" Her gaze drops to the soup in my palm, which my phone is balancing on precariously.

"Could you?" I nod toward the dangerous Jenga combo in my hand.

"Oh, yes," she says, grabbing my phone in one hand and the soup in the other.

I step inside and she closes her door behind me. She's still wearing what I assume she went to class in this morning, minus her sneakers. Whatever's going on must not be a head cold or a stomach bug because when Nikki gets those she wears the wallowing look well.

"Before you freak out, I'm covered. I logged in and it's the track coaches' day." She nods, knowing the inner workings of the Tiff sports staff fairly well, having been at my side for three years.

"Still, you didn't have to—"

I press my finger to her lips to halt her and lower my gaze.

"I wanted to come. Now, get in bed and let me take care of you," I command.

Her lips pucker into a bashful smile and she ekes out a soft, "Okay."

I fluff her blanket and build a backrest of pillows, then coax her to sit while I help remove the lid from the soup I brought.

"You have Fritos?" she asks when she notes the soup flavor. It's a tradition she and I have, and it drives our moms nuts. We add Fritos on top of everything, which they say is basically like putting ketchup on a gourmet steak. I'm pretty sure the café soup is far from gourmet. I think it's closer to mass canned.

I pull the bag of chips from my backpack and tear the top open with my teeth while she claps. I sprinkle a few onto the soup then climb into her bed to sit next to her with the rest of the bag.

"I don't think it's hot," I say, watching her blow on her first spoonful.

"You're right. It's *never* hot," she says, laughing. She takes her first bite, the Frito crunch bringing a bigger smile to her face.

"Best medicine ever?" I offer.

She nods.

I reach over and feel her head, checking for a fever, but she shakes her head and pushes my hand away.

"I'm not sick like that," she says.

I flush with instant sweat and feel the blood drain from my face as my mouth hangs open. Nikki takes another bite and turns her gaze to me, forehead crinkling when she sees my face, pausing with the spoon in her mouth. She studies me for a second, then her eyes flash wide.

"No! No, no, Alex. I am not pregnant. Jesus! Have you been talking to my mom?" She laughs at my conclusion, but I'm still trying to dig my heart out from the depths of my throat.

"I have an ear thing going on. Like an infection or something. I got drops," she says, motioning to a white paper bag on her desk.

"Oh, thank God! Because I'm not sure I can handle another bomb today. Not that you being . . . well . . . you're not a bomb, just—"

"Shhh," she says, pinching my lips closed. She wiggles her other finger at me. "Stop before you make it worse."

I smile, breaking free from her hand and pressing a kiss to her open palm.

"You said another bomb. What's the first bomb?" She offers me a bite of her soup, but I shake my head and dive into the extra Fritos.

"Seems the divorce is officially on.".

Nikki stops eating and turns her body into me.

"Alex, I'm really sorry." I hold her gaze for a second and see so many memories of both of our families together reflected in her eyes. It was rare that both our dads were together, hers being gone often for his job and mine living on the field at the high school. But when they were, it was always happy. Our households felt like one. And now, it feels like everything is crumbling. And I know part of Nikki feels that too.

She moves her bowl toward me. I take it from her and lean to my side to set it on her desk.

"I'll get used to it. And I know it's for the best. I mean, I'm shocked my mom started with the separation part but I don't really know how a divorce proceeding goes. Maybe she had to go through the steps." I shrug and wonder in an instant if this is what Nikki and my future will be. I shake the thought away fast, the mere presence of it terrifies me. Not the marrying her part but the separating stuff.

"I'm sure your mom did what was best for her and is doing what is best for you both," Nikki says, sliding down to rest her head in my lap.

I've taken care of her when she's sick before. But now,

she feels more precious. I run my hand through her hair and try to picture the scene in my head, my parents at the county courthouse handing over papers, signing, shaking. So cold and so quick. I'm not sure how long I let my mind wander, but when I look back down to my lap, Nikki's asleep.

I'm not sure which ear bothers her, but she probably should have put drops in before napping. The least I can do is get things ready for her and make sure she does it as soon as she wakes up. I slip out from under her and replace my leg with one of her pillows so I can unpackage her prescription from student health. The drops seem pretty cut and dried, but the bottle is enormous. When I have an ear infection, I usually get something about the size of a thimble. This thing rivals a travel shampoo.

I read the back, looking for the dosage, but pause on a very specific word—neuroma.

My pulse ratchets up. I reach for the bag again, holding it upside down and emptying the contents onto her desk. There's a stack of papers folded in half, so I start there. The first page looks like her discharge paperwork, and I see that word again. I pull my phone out and search the term, relieved when it comes up with another key word—benign. My heart slows again, but I'm still on edge as I read.

It's in her ear, and it causes vertigo, which makes sense. She's had a few issues with that lately, and she's also had some headaches. All of it feels digestible, and then I flip to the next page.

This is her bomb. A bomb of her own. That she was going to hold on to and protect and who knows what else —ignore, maybe? My eyes scan the header on the page.

HEARING LOSS FROM ACOUSTIC NEUROMA

I stumble back a step but catch myself before making a sound. I pull her chair out slowly from under her desk and continue reading. There's a lot of pages about surgery, and then a whole list of referrals. When I'm done, I fold the papers back as they were and tuck them inside her bag. I've broken about a million HIPAA laws, I'm sure, but how could I not? It's Nikki. It's Nikki's dream.

It's . . . it's Nikki.

I KNOW I've been quiet. I'm sure Alex senses it. Even before we became more, he could read me better than most. Better than all. I'm just not sure how to talk about it. It's all *so much*. It's more than a diagnosis from a visit to the student health center. It's life-altering. At least, it is for me. And Alex, he's got a game today. We're getting ready to leave, and I'm sitting here in his room like a miserable lump while he packs his gear.

"You ready?" He lifts my chin from my phone screen and I snap out of my daze at the sight of his eyes. His dimple. Ah, that get-out-of-jail-free card.

"Yeah, sorry. I was . . . spacing," I admit.

Really, I was searching for answers. Not about surgery, but about how people like me can still do what I want to do. Surgeries seem to be fifty-fifty. Some people have lost more hearing. Others have corrected the loss that's already come. Nobody goes back to being perfect, but maybe I wasn't perfect to begin with. I'm not sure how long this thing has been growing in my ear and changing me, but perhaps I've simply gotten used to it. And maybe what I hear isn't very good after all.

I take Alex's hand when we leave his house. Cole is already piled in the car, kindly taking the back seat so I can sit up front. That's something that hasn't changed. Cole has always pushed Alex and me together in subtle ways. Our moms would love him. Unless . . . oh man, did they get to him? That's something we're going to have to ask him when we come out. Which we still need to talk about.

I sigh, once again overwhelmed by my own chaos. There's so much.

"Hey, Nik." Cole reaches around from the back seat and hugs me from behind. I squeeze his hands, then glance to my left, where Alex is staring lasers into the rearview mirror.

"You okay?" I tilt my head, calculating where Alex's gaze is landing, pretty sure it's on Cole's forehead.

"I'm good. Yeah. Just something I have to do." Alex shifts in his seat, leaning his opposite elbow on the console so he can look Cole in the eyes.

"I thought we talked about . . . this," Alex says, waving his finger between me and him.

"Wait, Cole knows?" I shift to join the conversation, but the inside of a sedan is a really tight place to hash things out with three people.

Cole chuckles.

"I knew enough. But I wanted him to say it out loud in front of me. Mostly because—"

"Fine. You were right. Are you happy?" Alex's grumpiness seems to only make Cole laugh more, and he claps his hands together once and makes this really dorky swoony face.

"I've never been happier, my sweet Alex," he teases.

My face sours, and I push Alex out of the way to point a finger at Cole.

"Don't ever use that phrase again. I don't say that. Nobody says that. That's . . . weird. So stop." I shake my head, then move to meet Alex's gaze. "Am I right?"

"Oh, you're right. Very weird," Alex says.

We both nod and I lean over the console the remaining few inches to give him a quick peck before buckling up. Cole remains silent for a few seconds.

"Gee," he finally breaks through. "I see what you like so much about her."

The dead silence that follows lasts only a few seconds, but soon the three of us erupt in laughter. It feels good. And for the short ride to the stadium, I don't think about anything besides the many ways I plan to torture Alex with *my sweet Alex* in the coming days.

I kiss him one more time before he heads toward the fieldhouse with Cole, and I catch him telling Cole to shut up as they walk away. I hover by the main gates, trying new searches on my phone while I wait for Omar and Brian to meet me. I finally find one article about a professor in Indiana who works in the sound engineering department and he's nearly deaf. It's more of a human interest piece, but for me the takeaway is the power of the visuals in the technology. It seems the professor was a roadie with a pretty famous band for years in the seventies and eighties. Lax safety precautions destroyed his hearing, but he found that working with the same musicians for so long gave him a certain feel for when things were right.

"It's those unteachable instincts," he said in the story. "I can rest my palms on the board and feel when something is off. And now, thanks to technology, I can see it."

"What's so engrossing?" Omar says, startling me as he pops up behind me.

I jump and fumble my phone.

"Was just reading, waiting on your late ass," I tease, not ready to talk to him about my news. I will, however, share the more exciting news with him.

"So, how was your weekend? Anything . . . new?" My voice lifts up at the end, a character trait definitely weird for me, and Omar notes it as we walk.

"Why are you smiling like that?" His eyes dim while Brian looks at me, amused.

"Oh, she had sex," Brian says, and I was not quite prepared for his bluntness. Neither, it seems, was Omar, as we both cup our mouths with our hands and stare at each other with wide eyes.

Omar points at me across his boyfriend's body while Brian chuckles, proud of himself for solving the riddle so fast.

"You're not denying it!" Omar's shouting is barely muffled by his other hand, which still covers his mouth.

I drop my hands, sure my face is beet red, and shake my head slightly.

"I am not denying it."

Omar's hand drops long enough to glimpse the large O formed by his lips. My face does the same, and soon we're both back to hiding behind hands.

"You two are schoolchildren," Brian teases. I'm getting a Coke. Save my seat.

As soon as Brian leaves us, Omar pulls me to him as we walk toward our seats.

"It's happened," he says.

I nod.

"It's happened a few times," I admit.

More hands over faces, and now we've added giggling.

I stop when I spot Alicia, this time here alone, without her posse. Why is she here? My chest tightens, but Omar is quick to shake me—literally, though gently. "Do not go there, Nikki. You had sex a few times," he repeats my words back to me.

I shoot him a grin.

"I did, didn't I?"

Feeling more confident and a little like bragging, I decide to step over the seats this time rather than endure passing by my least favorite person at Tiff. I give her a wave that she sneers at, then slump down in my seat. Omar strategically positions himself between her and me —along with the dozen or so other seats I've built into the barrier.

"Oh, she's going to hate you," he says.

"Good, it's mutual."

"So, spill it. Does this mean you two are a thing? Did you drop the big L? What did he say? I want play-by-play, though not sure I need to know about your skivvies and junk," he says, sprinkling his fingertips in the air over my crotch.

"Omar!" My mouth widens as I chastise him.

He shrugs, and I do my best to cool my body temperature. I must be glowing red.

"We haven't really talked about, I don't know, *terms?*" I'm not sure what words to use here, but that one feels too legal.

"Okay, so you aren't defining things just yet. That's okay."

I sigh.

"Is it?" I look out on the field, catching Alex's gaze. He tips his hat and my chest warms as I lift my palm.

"Nik, you've been imagining for years how all this would go down. It doesn't have to fall into place all at once. But"—he stops and literally takes my hand in his, closing it between both of his. It's strange for him to be serious like this. I meet his eyes—"You have to make sure you tell him how you truly feel. Not just the lust part, but the love part."

My shoulders hike up.

"I don't want to overwhelm him. I'm so happy that we're here, and that we clearly both have feelings. Love is a big leap."

And just to prove why he's my friend, he echoes my words right back in my face.

"Is it?"

IT'S a miracle I'm able to follow the game. My mind is spring boarding between my own problems, the advice from Omar, and the new problem playing out on the field—Alex isn't at shortstop. Coach moved him to the outfield today, giving Edwin a start at short.

"Is he really going to be that upset?" Omar asks.

"Yes," both Brian and I say at the same time. We make eyes, and I'm glad Omar is dating an athlete because he gets it. I'm sure there are similar pressures in lacrosse.

Alex managed a base hit for his first at bat. Nothing memorable but a solid slap down the line. His speed stands out, like it always does. And he's made some good plays in the outfield. But as he goes through the motions outside the dugout, taking practice hacks off to the side, I see the forces starting to crush him. And all it does is make me wonder if he's noticed the man sitting by himself far along the third base side.

Alex Sr. showed up alone about twenty minutes ago. He's wearing his Tiff jacket, which is unique enough that it draws eyes. If he's in view of the dugout, there's no way Alex hasn't noticed him.

I lean forward in my seat, scanning between Senior and Junior. Alex is first up for the inning. He digs his back foot in and hovers his bat over the plate. It's a different look for him, different from his last at bat, which was also different from his norm. He's trying things, which is common for guys going through slumps. But nothing is landing. It's getting him through, but everything looks so uncomfortable.

Whatever his thought process was for this new approach, it was wrong, because he swings at the first pitch and sends the ball straight up for an easy out with the catcher. I hold my breath and suck in my bottom lip, willing Alex to keep his cool as he walks back into the dugout. I flinch at the sound of metal clanking against wood, and I can't help but glance back at his father after Alex threw his bat into the rack. Senior never tolerated that type of outburst on his field—in his son. "Emotions are good," he would say. "But tantrums? Those are for babies."

I watch as his father rubs his hands over his face and shifts in his chair.

"I'll be right back," I say to Omar and Brian.

I skip over the seats and walk along the concourse to the other side, making my way down the last row of steps until I'm right next to the man, who in many ways, had a part in raising me.

"Hi," I say, getting his attention.

"Nikki!" His genuine excitement to see me feels nice, and he leaps to his feet then swallows me in a hug. It feels like a betrayal, but I throw my arms around his back and reciprocate.

"How are you?" he asks, scooting over a seat so I can sit next to him. I check the view, a little relieved that one of the light poles obscures us slightly. I'm sure Alex has noticed, regardless.

"I've been good," I say, which isn't a total lie. I have been good. I've been great. I've also been a fucking mess. "You?"

We meet eyes for an awkward second, and I quickly glance away.

"Sorry, I didn't mean—"

"It's okay."

We watch the field for a few seconds in silence.

"Alex isn't good," I finally utter. But he knows that.

"That's my fault."

"*Mmm*," I agree.

The next two batters strike out, so at least Alex made contact. I know he'll look for me when he gets to the field, if he hasn't already.

"Why'd you come?" I swivel my head to look at him when I ask.

He takes a deep breath, his arms crossed over the TIFF logo on his jacket, his face marked by tan lines from the glasses he usually wears. They're propped on his head right now.

"I don't miss a game. Been watching them online. Saw fall ball too."

I nod.

"Okay, but you came in person." I know why he's here, but I want him to say it. And then he needs to find a way to say it to Alex so his son can let go and listen long enough to get what he needs.

"He's struggling. His stance is all wrong. His at bats have been—"

"He's been shit. He knows that," I say, wincing a little at calling him out on it bluntly.

"I know he knows. He might not think I know him, but I still do. I always will. At least out here. This is the one place . . ."

"The one place you still want a relationship," I finish.

He sighs, then rolls his head to the side to meet my gaze.

"Yeah, I guess so."

"What should I tell him?" I'm certain he knows what I mean by that question. I don't need to know what to say about him being here, or about life, or about how sorry he is. I need the small nugget. The piece of wisdom. I need the thing that works. That has always worked.

He chews at his lips, his mouth so much like his son's. They share the same dimple, though his is permanent now, weathered from sun and wrinkled with age.

"Tell him to cut the field in half. Stand quiet. Crack the whip and commit."

I repeat his words in my head.

"Okay," I say, standing but placing my hand on his shoulder. It's a hard space to navigate with him—to have old fondness and new hate.

I head back to my seat and plop down next to Omar, feeling both his and Brian's eyes on me. I glance at Omar and give him the tight smile I do when I don't want to talk about something.

"Okay. Later, maybe," he says.

I nod and look back to the field.

"Later, but definitely." I'm going to need to talk to someone about this mess, and it can't be Alex.

Tiff ends up losing by two runs, and the new pitcher, the one I saw buckle Alex's knees during practice, was the one to blow the small lead we had. I'm a little smug about it. He might be a nice guy, but the fact he kicked Alex when he was already down, so to speak, puts him on my shit list.

Alex's dad left before the ninth. I'm relieved. This is going to be difficult as it is because I'm sure Alex saw us talking. I send Brian and Omar to Patty's without me and take a seat on a folding chair one of the coaches left just outside the clubhouse. Alicia is lingering by the gate. I want to tell her she's been cut loose, but also, she's not my concern right now. Alex is.

He's one of the first to exit for once, which catches me off-guard. He doesn't spot me right away and starts to walk in the other direction, scouring the walkways that circle the field.

"I'm right here," I say.

He spins around fast, and his expression isn't what I expect at all.

"Oh, I figured you'd be giving my dad a tour or something."

"Alex, what?" My mouth hangs open, and his lips pull tight as he steps in close, his eyes narrowing.

"That was a pretty long chat. Nice welcome hug. How is the old man?" His tone is curt. He's hot, which I did expect. Just . . . not . . . *this* hot.

"He's been watching your games at home. He wanted to help. And—"

I know the words aren't coming out right as I utter them. I prepared what to say, but in the heat of the moment, it all jumbles.

"Ohhhh, he wanted to help. He should have stayed home, then. Hope you didn't invite him to my next game," he says, turning his back to me. He starts to walk toward the gate and I follow.

"Wait a second, that's not fair," I utter.

Alex turns around but continues moving away.

"You know what? I'm just in a mood. I had another shit game. I got moved to the outfield. I might not even play tomorrow, and now my best friend is cozying up to the guy who ruined my life. I just . . . I need a minute." He holds his palms out, then lets them fall to his sides.

I stop, letting the distance between us grow.

"You need a minute?" For whatever reason, my mind replays his dad's advice. It's locked in there. Why is that what I'm remembering?

"I told Alicia I'd give her a ride home. I'll . . . let me go

home, shower, get my shit together. I'll . . . I'll text you."
He spins around and continues his walk.

I have a lot of my mother in me, but my temper? That comes from my dad. There's a reason he's in a job where he doesn't have to talk to people often, where he's essentially in charge. Because discourse? Not his thing.

Without missing a beat, I pull my sneaker from my right foot and throw it at Alex as hard as I can. It smacks him in the center of his back, a vivid dirt-colored shoe print left in its wake. Alex stops and turns around to stare at my shoe.

"Nikki, what the fuck? Did you throw your shoe at me?" He holds his palms out again, which pulls my dad's traits out even more. I pull my other shoe off and throw it at his head. He deflects it and it goes tumbling down a small grass ravine.

"You're being nuts!" He bends down and picks up my shoe, then marches to the other one before carrying them both back to me, dropping them at my feet.

My nostrils flex.

"You're taking Alicia home?" I point at her over his shoulder. She sees me, so I give her the middle finger.

"Jesus, Nik. She doesn't have a ride." He shakes his head, then bites the tip of his tongue. "You . . . you hugged my dad."

His voice cracks with that last bit. I knew it would be a risk to talk to him in front of Alex, but I did anyway. I did it to help him. Though now that I'm in the middle of this fight with him, I'm not sure what reasoning made me follow through with it. It was a bad idea.

"I'll call you after I drop her off," he finally says, dropping his hand the same way his dad used to do when he was done with a conversation. I open my mouth to point it out but stop myself because too many ironies have already piled up.

I'm too pissed to cry. And I know Alex isn't going to do anything but take Alicia home. He wouldn't. He's not that guy. When he was with Alicia, he was faithful. Even when she wasn't always. In high school, he was the best boyfriend to every girl but me. He's a good man with a good heart and a lot of instant baggage and stress. But also, he knows that taking Alicia home right now is a slap in my face. And he's doing that because I talked to Senior.

"Hey, you're still here," Brayden says from behind me. I shut my eyes as he's the last person I want to see right now.

"I was just leaving," I say, starting to walk. Alex's car is pulling from the lot. I'm sure Brayden sees. I bet he loves that.

"Wait up," he calls from behind me. I don't slow, but it doesn't stop him from jogging to catch up. He matches my gait.

"Brayden, we don't have to do this—"

"I'm sorry," he cuts in.

I glance to my right and shoot him a skeptical expression.

His mouth drops into a flat line and he shakes his head.

"No, I'm being sincere. I'm sorry. I wanted to apologize for being a major asshole at the party. And we don't have to be friends. Just, please accept that from me."

I stop walking for a beat, and he halts as well.

Alex's truck is long gone, but even still, talking to Brayden feels gross. It feels like a betrayal.

"Okay, Brayden. I accept your apology. But you owe one to Alex. And I'm not going to let that go."

He holds my gaze for a second, and I catch the short laugh he lets slip, but I think he sees in my eyes how serious I am. Finally, he nods.

"Okay, Nik. I'll work on that." He holds out his hand, and I smirk and let my own little laugh slip. We shake, but I know in my gut he won't work on shit.

"You going to Patty's?" I ask.

"I am," he answers.

"Good. You can buy my beer."

We walk the four blocks in silence, and sometimes I'm a few steps ahead. But I let him keep up with me. And I'm doing that because Alex took Alicia home.

Maybe that's what he has been warning me about with *us*. When you cross lines, people get hurt. If we were just friends, this wouldn't burn through me the way it is. I still would have talked to his dad, though. Because that move? That was friend Nikki doing him a solid. And he'll realize that eventually.

NIKKI DIDN'T DESERVE THAT. And she also had every right to question me taking Alicia home. It was a dick move.

Not wanting to completely incinerate my karma, I come clean to Alicia as I pull up to her apartment building.

"You should know, Nikki and I? We . . . we're together now." It's strange that other than Cole, she's the only person I've told. How wrong is that?

She laughs at first but I give her a look that admonishes her, my mouth drawn in on one side and my eyes narrowed.

"I'm sorry. You're actually together, huh?"

She knows I was serious the first time.

"We are." I shrug.

She looks out my windshield and blinks a few times with her mouth hung open.

"Wow. I actually called it. All those years ago, when I made you kiss?" She blinks her way back to me.

I start to argue but then decide maybe she needs this to save face. I'm not out to crush her façade. She can do that on her own.

"Yep. You did. I mean, if we never kissed back then, who knows." I shrug again, but deep down? I know. Nikki knows. We would have kissed eventually. I'm coming around on just how inevitable we are.

"For what it's worth, I always thought you looked like you fit." She reaches across the console and squeezes my forearm, her words almost a compliment, but not quite.

"Thanks," I say, and she slips out the passenger side and scurries up the stairs to her apartment door. I wait to make sure she gets inside, then flip the car around to head home so I can shower and get my head on straight.

I've been putting off calling my mom, and I could probably use her wisdom right now, so I press call on the Bluetooth. She answers after the second ring.

"Mijo. How was your game?" She doesn't always watch. It makes her nervous.

"It was all right," I say. I haven't been telling her about my struggles; she has enough going on. She should know about *him* though.

"Dad showed up," I say.

I told her I asked him not to come for a while. She never reacted to that news either way.

"Well, he loves you. He's a really terrible husband, but he is so proud of you."

I laugh out hard.

"What? Don't laugh at me, that isn't nice."

"No, no. It's just that . . . it's such a cliché thing to say. *Mom and Dad are splitting up, but we both love you very much.* I'm twenty-two. I don't need the kid gloves."

"Ah, baby boy," she says, that mocking tone only she can get away with. I settle into my seat and relax more, my hand slung over the wheel as I slow down. "You will always need kid gloves."

I chuckle.

"Perhaps."

I don't really want to be filled in on how court went, so I let her fill me in on her day. She has an advanced class of students this year, and they've been reinvigorating her love of teaching. It's nice to hear her talk about her work like this. For years, it's always sounded exhausting—parents yelling at her for reading choices, students cheating and getting caught. This year seems to be low on the negatives, at least professionally.

"And how is Nikki?"

I smirk at her tone. It's always there, every time she asks about Nik.

"She's good," I say.

Silence builds for a few seconds.

"Alex, is there something on your mind?" she asks.

I replay my tone in my own head, and I don't think there was any way she could read me and know that Nikki and I have gotten together. Maybe she just has that *mom* thing. Sixth sense. Eyes on the back of the head. Wiretaps.

"Yeah," I sigh out.

"Lay it on me, son," she says, and I hear the porch chair slide on concrete. She's getting into advice mode, which is good. I need some.

"You know how you and Julianne are always meddling," I start.

"What? We don't meddle," she says, her tone clear that she knows they do.

"Yeah, *mmm hmm*. Okay. Anyhow, you know what I mean. You two have always sort of pushed—"

"Gently nudged," she corrects. She sounds excited, and that makes me feel a little scared.

"Right, well, the nudging. We maybe, finally, sort of—"

"No!" she shouts. I turn my speaker volume down because it crackles.

I sigh, but not in a negative way. It feels good to tell her. Good to be with Nik.

"Yes, you and Auntie Julianne can gloat all you want. We maybe kissed, and have been hanging out." My mom's not stupid, but I sure as hell am not giving her details.

"I knew it! I knew this day would come. And I knew it would be soon."

"Yeah, okay. Well, before I end something before it really starts, I need your help. I maybe, sort of, kinda . . . fucked up."

"Alex." She says my name sternly. Probably both because of my language and because I did, well, fuck up.

"I know. Sorry. I just . . . I've been under some stress, and baseball season is always full of pressure, and then

Dad showed up today. I kind of took that out on Nikki." I hold my breath and wait for her to give me the magic advice she always does. But the longer the silence goes on, the more my stomach hurts.

"Mom?" *Is she still there?*

"I'm here. I don't know what to tell you. You love her. You go tell her you're sorry, and then you put in the work."

"Yeah, I've always loved her. I get that. But now it's different," I try to explain, but she cuts me off.

"No, no. You aren't hearing me. Yeah, you've loved her. But now you realize you are *in* love with her. And Alex, you've been in love with her for a lot longer than you know. And she's been in love with you right back."

Shit. Has she? Have I? *I definitely have.*

"You thought you were in love with Dad," I say before my personal gatekeeping kicks in. "Sorry, I didn't mean that like that."

"No, you're right. And I still love your dad. But I'm no longer *in* love. And really, we are both to blame. Him more, of course."

I laugh with her.

"When you are so close to someone that you share air, space, time, dreams, plans—children—it is not always smooth sailing. You can't both always have good days. You'll be out of sync. And you'll lash out. And you'll be right, and you'll be wrong. But at the end of the day, you find each other, and you say the words that mean the most. You get the ugly stuff out of your system and remind each other that you love one another. Somewhere along the way, your dad quit coming in at the end of the day to talk it out. He quit reminding me. And I willingly forgot. And then—"

She likely made some gesture just now, waving a hand off in the wind I imagine.

"Okay, so I should probably find Nik is what you're saying." I pull into the driveway and let the car idle.

"You know the answer to that," she says.

I breathe out a short laugh.

"Yeah, I do. Thanks, Mom. I love you."

"I love you, too. And make sure you two come home for break. They're having a big sale at the outlet."

That fucking bread outlet. I laugh to myself as I back out of the driveway. I pause in the middle of the street and press call on Nikki's contact info. It goes right to voice-mail so I dial again. The same result. She's really pissed.

I head to her place and talk out a quick text on my way.

ME: I'm so sorry. I'm coming over. Let's talk.

First, we'll talk about us. I'm going to tell her exactly how I feel, how terrified I am that we'll turn into my parents, and how hard I'm going to work to never let that happen. Then I want her to tell me about why she talked to my dad. I know it wasn't to be cruel. And maybe he does really give a damn. I'm sure he loves me. It's just so hard to get past what he did, and I'm not quite ready to listen to him. Maybe, though, maybe I can listen to *her*.

And then when I'm done, I'm going to urge her to tell me on her own about her hearing. And if she can't or won't, I'm going to make sure she knows that whatever is going on in her life, she doesn't face it alone. She has me. Always.

I'm never going anywhere.

I pull into the dorm lot and shift into park just as my phone buzzes. My heart is pounding with nerves and adrenaline, and I almost call her rather than read the text she just sent. But then I catch the name.

Brayden.

That's not a text from her.

I swipe my phone.

BRAYDEN: Took Nikki to dinner at Patty's. She seemed upset. Was that Alicia I saw you leave with?

That motherfucker!

I toss my phone into the passenger seat and peel out in reverse while I fumble my seat belt back in place. I'm in the Patty's lot in under a minute, not even sure if I turned the car off or shut my door by the time I bust through the entry doors and zero in on Brayden.

"You really must love getting punched in the face," I say to his back.

My fist is ready to swing as he turns around, but before I can take a crack at him, Nikki walks out from the restroom and sits down at a table across the room next to Cutter and his girlfriend. Her phone is on the table. She didn't even see my calls.

"You know what? You're not worth it," I drop my hand and start to move past him.

"I hear they moved in together, by the way. Your dad

and my cousin? I bet you didn't know that part yet." I stop, still within striking distance, and let my jaw pop. My molars press together hard enough to crack while my hand flexes at my side.

But then, she sees me.

Nikki's gaze cuts right through the crowded bar, across a dozen tables filled with beer and loud ballplayers and sorority girls and frat boys. She rises above the noise, and my body relaxes.

I turn my head to Brayden, who is clearly sitting alone —now that my wits let me take in the context clues. I reach into my wallet and pull out a twenty, tossing it on the table.

"Good for them. This round's on me to celebrate. Enjoy."

I shove my wallet back into my workout pants, then beeline through the crowd to Nikki. Before she has a chance to open her mouth, I lift her from her stool and toss her over my shoulder like I did in high school.

"Alex Mendoza, what are you doing?" She swats at my back, open-palmed, and her hits are landing hard. I'm sure there are prints left behind, but I can handle it.

"I'm taking you to my bed," I say, loud enough that Cutter, his girlfriend Laney, and half the damn bar hears me. I gather up her wallet and phone, tucking them into the front of my hoodie, then face Cole at the next table.

"Atta boy," he says, and we high-five.

"You are not seriously doing this. Alex, put me down!" She's pulling at my waistband, a move she's had for years.

She's smart. She always gives me wedgies when I lift her this way. She's not gentle.

"Gentlemen," I say, saluting a few of the guys to my right.

The immediate crowd starts to cheer, which only eggs Nikki on more. She manages to grab a beer from one of the tables as I snake our way through the bar, and pours it down the back of my leg. I laugh, though it's pretty fucking cold.

It gets quiet once I exit Patty's and even quieter when the door slams shut behind me. I march to my car, which, yup—is still running. I carry her to the passenger side and open the door while she kicks and flails. I finally put her down because wrangling her into this seat is like putting a cat in a sample cup of water.

She smacks my chest with her palms.

"I'm still mad at you, Alex Mendoza!" She's practically growling, but also, there's a flicker in her eyes.

"Yeah, well, I love you, Nikki Thomas," I say back.

In a half second, her expression morphs from one ready to spit fire at me into a wide-eyed girl in shock. I nod.

"Yeah, I love you. I'm sorry I got pissy and took my shit out on you. And I'm sorry it took me years to tell you. But I love you. And I think maybe you love me. So, there it is. Be mad at me. Let me have it. And when you're done, I'd really like to fucking kiss you."

nikki

"WELL, DAMMIT."

How can I be this mad yet want to grin ear to ear?

"Go on. Let me have it," Alex says again.

I reach up and grab the strings on his hoodie and wrap them around my palms while I look him in the eyes, my tongue poking the inside of my cheek.

"How can I let you have it when you hit me with a speech like that? Gah! Fine." I shake the strings against him and look to the side, where a few people are peeking through the Patty's door. "You really just told all those people you were about to take me to bed."

"I did," he says.

"Welp"—I let the P pop. I shift my eyes back to him—"Wouldn't want to let them down."

His fucking dimple appears. I step into him, lifting on my toes, and his hands clutch the sides of my head as his mouth crashes into mine. It's a hungry kiss, and it's possessive. A public declaration that borders on an R rating by the time he pulls away. A whistle in the distance draws our attention, and Cole cups his mouth and shouts, "Yeah, buddy!"

My palm nudges Alex's focus back to me.

"I assume he meant that for me," I say, and his raspy laugh is the sexiest sound I've heard, maybe ever.

"I love you, too, by the way," I say, dropping into the passenger seat. He gives me a crooked smile as he hangs on the door.

"Yeah? You saying I was right?"

"Tsssk, always so cocky," I tease. "I loved you first, so no. I'm not saying that at all."

His head waggles side to side.

"Kinda feels like I called it, though," he says, one eye squinted, a playful arrogance in his expression.

I reach toward him and cup his hard-on, which seems to get his attention.

"I mean, you were first. And right. You ready?" He closes my door without waiting for my answer, and when he slips into the driver's seat, I put my hand right back where it was. And Alex, he blows through his first red light and gets pulled over about twenty seconds from home.

I bite my thumb while he fumbles through his glove box under the beam of the officer's mega flashlight.

"I'm sorry," I whisper, knowing this is my fault.

"It's fine. I just need my, oh . . . yeah . . . there it is," he says, pulling a pile of papers out and sifting through them in my lap. I start to giggle, and he hushes me, but there's a smirk on his face. I'm glad he's finding the humor in this too.

He finds his registration finally and hands it to the officer.

"I'll be right back," she says, and heads back to her car to run his ID.

"Oh, my God!" I break out in a whisper once we're in the clear. Alex leans his elbow on the window sill and covers his face while he laughs.

"I swear to God, Nikki, if this lady makes me get out and walk a straight line, I am screwed."

I bunch my brow at him but then realize what he means. His workout pants are sporting an enormous bulge. I'm a little impressed that the panic of being pulled over didn't ruin things for him.

"*Shh! Shh!* She's coming back," I say as I stare out the back window.

"Mr. Mendoza?"

"Yes, ma'am."

The officer leans in, a move I assume is partly a smell test to see if he's been drinking. Her eyes meet mine and I freeze, offering what I hope looks like a guilty smile. A few long seconds pass, and I'm not one hundred percent on this, but I think she got the picture.

"Here's your license. Put this back in the glove box. Maybe clean that out, too," she says, shining her light on the pile of papers strewn around the console.

"Yes, ma'am," Alex says, his hands shaking while he puts his license back in place.

"Pay attention. I know there aren't a lot of people on the street right now, but people aren't always easy to see. Red lights are there for a reason." She pats the top of the car and moves on.

"Yes, thank you. Thank you, officer. Than—"

I grab his wrist.

"She got it." We look at each other for a beat, then bust into more laughter.

Once I shove Alex's paper collection back into the glove box and the cop pulls away, he drives us the rest of the way to his house, never going a mile over the speed limit. When he slips the gear into park, though, he's all about speed, darting out of the car and flinging my door open. He grabs my hand and tugs me to my feet, not bothering to carry me this time. He doesn't have to. At this point, he can race me up those stairs.

We're in his bedroom with the door closed in seconds, and our clothes are in a pile on the floor a few breaths later. This time feels different. It feels familiar and spontaneous. Like two people in love, making love.

I lay back in the center of his bed and Alex takes my foot in his hand, caressing it and kissing the top. He crawls onto the bed, on his knees, still holding my leg and kissing the inside of my calf next.

"You have really sexy legs, you know that?" He sets my right leg down and pulls my knees up, running his hands over both of them, then sliding them down the insides of my thighs. He comes close to touching me but backs off, and I whimper.

"Always so anxious," he teases.

"You really like my legs?" I never really think much of them myself. He traces along my shins then lets his hands roam the same path again, this time letting the tips of his fingers tease my swollen center for the briefest of seconds. I lift my hips and he pulls away.

"I love your legs, Nikki," he says, bending down to kiss my knee before pushing my legs apart, flattening them on the bed.

"I love hearing you say that word," I hum.

Love. Love. Love. Love.

"Good," he says, "because I love a lot of things about you."

He lowers himself, settling between my legs and kissing the inside of my thigh. He tickles my skin with his knuckles then moves to the other leg, doing the same.

"I love this part of you right here," he says, his tongue taking a small taste. "You have these freckles that line up, they look like the Little Dipper," he says, tracing the constellation with his fingertip. I writhe, wanting him to move his finger higher.

"Yeah?" I let out in a soft cry.

"*Mmm hmm,*" he says, kissing me there again.

"And I love this part of you, right here," he says, resting his wrists on my hip bones and brushing his fingertips along the small trail of hair that I am so thankful I spent time on this morning.

"Yeah?" I cry, lifting my hips. He quickly presses them back down.

"Yeah," he answers, sliding his body upward enough to press a kiss on my pelvis.

"And your belly button, and this stud that I called stupid," he says, tapping it with his finger.

I lift my head and look him in the eyes. They crinkle and I know he's smiling. I can't see his mouth, though, because it's too busy being so fucking close to where I want it.

"And your . . ." He exhales, his breath tickling my pussy. I moan just before his tongue flicks my clit, then yelp in pleasure.

"Yeah, I love this pussy, Nikki. I fucking love the way it tastes," he says, taking a more forceful pass with his tongue this time. My eyes roll back, and I drop my head back to the bed.

"I love the way it gets so swollen when you think about me," he says, pushing a finger inside.

"Alex," I moan.

He pushes in a second finger and licks my clit.

"And I love the way you say my name when I taste this pussy," he says, his mouth moving against me.

"Alex," I say again, hoping to be rewarded.

He pulls his fingers out and sucks me in, his tongue punishing my clit and forcing me to whimper for relief.

"I love how wet you get for me," he says, lifting up to his knees again.

I bring my knees up and lift my hips, hoping . . . wanting. *Begging.*

Alex grips his cock and slides the tip up and down the

length of my pussy, teasing me and almost entering me several times until, finally, he pulls my legs up with his arms and pushes in.

"Ahhh!" I gasp.

"Fuck, do I love this view," he says, sliding out slowly.

"What view?" I ask, wanting to hear the filthy words fall from his lips.

He pushes in again, harder. Deeper.

"My cock in your pussy," he says, pulling out completely. He teases me more with his finger, then shoves in again with his penis. I push my hips up to meet him.

"I love your cock in my pussy, too," I say, urging him to move more.

I grip the bedding at my sides and lift my chin, meeting his eyes as his hips thrust back and forth. His hands hold my legs as he pumps into me faster and we chase our release. I feel mine building and I buck my hips, wanting him to drive in deeper.

The sound of skin on skin fills the room as his body smacks against mine, his cock hitting me so deep and hard that I lose my breath when the first wave hits. My body quakes from the way he punishes my pussy, relentless and hungry. As I peak, he drops my legs and shifts me so he can cage me between his arms and thrust into me with more force, filling me with his hot cum then collapsing on top of me from sheer, wonderful exhaustion.

I run my fingertips along his sticky back, his skin slick with sweat. I kiss his shoulder and taste the salt. He lifts his head and brushes my hair from my face, then sucks in my upper lip.

"I love that fucking lip too, by the way," he says.

I suck it in and he instantly pulls it out.

"No. Never hide that. That lip is the reason I fell in love with you."

My eyes pull in.

"My . . . lip? All of this"—I run my hand along my side from hip to ear—"and you like the lip."

He presses a soft kiss to it again and shakes his head.

"No, Nikki. I love the lip. And I love you."

I DIDN'T WANT Nikki to have to wake up at the crack of dawn again to get back to her dorm room in time, so after I made sure she knew exactly how many parts of her I loved, and there were *so many*, we both showered then packed me a bag to stay with her.

I've been watching her get ready for bed, the meticulous way she brushes her hair, cleans her face, and puts on those fucking sexy little shorts. She also spent some time flipping through papers I recognized on her desk, and now she's crawling into bed to rest on her side while she lets the ear drops do their thing for five minutes.

Please talk to me about it. Please.

"Does it tickle?" I ask as she dabs in a few droplets.

"A little." She giggles.

I take the bottle from her and recap it as she nestles into the pillow. I set the drops on the edge of her desk and sink in next to her so I can run my fingers through her hair. I think this might be the cure to my anxieties. I could do this every night and feel sane. Something about the silkiness of her hair, the way it slips through my fingers, is soothing. It helps that her eyelids usually get heavy, too, and then I get to watch her sleep.

"Can we talk about something?" she starts.

My chest tightens, but not in a nervous way. Maybe a little tepid, but mostly hopeful.

"Of course," I say, kissing the tip of her nose.

Her eyes scrunch up and she smiles.

"I know we said we love each other, but Alex, I mean it. I love you. I've loved you for years. You can ask Omar."

My eyes widen.

"Wow, Omar knew before me?"

She narrows her eyes and puckers her lips.

"You knew."

I shrug slightly. Maybe I did. But I didn't let myself really believe it. I kept it at arm's length. Safe. Or so I thought. Nothing was safe about that, though. It was more like torture. Think of what we've missed.

"I love you too, Nikki. And not in the rushed, horny, college guy who wants to fuck way."

"*Mmm*, romantic, Alex."

I laugh softly and continue stroking her hair.

"I'm bad with words sometimes. I just mean, I didn't say all that in the bar for show. I said it for you. To you. Because it's you, Nik. It's you and me. And how lucky am I?" I lean in and kiss my favorite lip again, holding on to it, letting my tongue glide across it as she hums against me.

"I'm not going anywhere," I say.

"Me neither," she adds.

An incredible sense of peace fills my body. My pulse settles into this rhythm, my lungs clear and full. I believe it. I believe in us.

I hold her gaze for almost a minute. It's a nice quiet. Comfortable, like looking out upon calm waters.

She blinks slowly and takes a deep breath.

"I have something wrong with my ear," she says.

I don't stop my hand movement. I keep running it through her hair while I think. I could let her go through the story and tell me from the beginning, or I could save her from that. At the very least.

"I know," I admit.

She sucks in her lips, and I decide that just this once, she can keep that upper lip and hold on to it for a moment.

"You saw?" Her eyes glance up, toward her desk.

I nod.

"I'm scared."

I nod slowly.

"I know," I say again.

Her timer sounds from her phone and she sits up, tipping her head the other way and pushing a small ball of cotton into her ear. She leaves it in place and folds her legs to sit up. I prop my head on my elbow.

"Have you called the surgeon yet, just to talk? It might help to actually talk to the expert and get your questions answered."

"I haven't," she admits. "And I need to get the CT scan."

I know she knows the reasons she should, but also, I get being afraid to know too much. I was afraid I tore my labrum in high school, so I put off telling anyone for days. It ended up being all right, and I spent two weeks feeling sick and terrified for no reason.

This isn't quite the same. Nikki already knows she has a neuroma. She already has some hearing loss. But maybe finding out what's available after diagnosis will help ease her fears.

"Okay, how about this," I say, reaching up and touching my fingertips to her chin. "If you make an appointment to see what your options are, I'll . . ." I take in a deep breath, giving myself one last chance to back out of this.

"You'll go with me?" Nikki says.

"Of course," I respond, lifting myself up and kissing her softly.

Her shoulders relax, but only a little.

I'm off the hook, but that wasn't what I was going to say. And because it's Nikki, omitting feels a whole lot like lying.

"What I was going to say is if you make that call, I'll go talk to my dad."

My chest fills with concrete, but in an instant, it clears as Nikki leans in and kisses me this time. Her cool hands rest on my cheeks as she holds her lips to mine. And when she pulls away, she smiles like she's proud.

"You'll see him today?" she asks.

And there's the concrete again. My mouth gets dry and my lips part despite absolutely no words at the ready.

"Alex."

"I know." I roll to my back and pinch the bridge of my nose. Nikki leans over me, folding her arms on my chest and propping her chin on her fist.

"You know what he told me at your game?" she offers.

My eyes puzzle. I forgot that I never let her finish that part. I'm fucking stubborn sometimes.

"What?" I ask.

"He said to tell you to cut the field in half. Stand quiet. Crack the whip and commit."

I blink, a little impressed that she nailed it. I'm sure that's what he said. Those exact words. And hearing them now takes me back to being ten and standing in the batter's box while a kid twice my size revs up to throw a fastball past my face.

"Cut the field in half. Stand quiet. Crack the whip and commit." That's what my dad said then, and I hit my first homerun over the fence. He never let up, either. That became the routine. It's how I led the division in high school batting averages. How I knocked in more runs than anyone in Odell history. It's what got me to Tiff.

"You aren't going to get out of your slump until you walk through this fire," she says.

And damn if she isn't right.

I **SEND** the text from the stadium parking lot. My game isn't for six hours and I got out of my business ethics class early. I honestly think Nikki went to her accounting class as a way to force my hand. It's not like I can spend these hours with her. Not *all* of them at least.

A few minutes pass with no response, so I start my engine with a touch of relief that I'm off the hook for now. My phone buzzes in the cup holder as soon as I shift into reverse. I slam the shifter back into park and let my head fall against the headrest while I let out a heavy laugh.

I glance down where my phone rests, the alert obvious. There's his name, SENIOR. It's always been Senior. I gnaw at my lip, a slight voice somewhere in the back of my head telling me to pretend I don't see it. To leave. To go home and take a long, hot shower and then rest for an hour.

To disappoint Nikki.

I groan as I snatch my phone and swipe to read his response. I asked if he was still in town.

SENIOR: I am. Would you like lunch? On me.

I snort out a laugh. That's the least he owes me after all this. Fucker better have five-star meals delivered to Mom for the next ten years too.

I'm not really hungry, so I come up with an alternative.

ME: Not hungry. Can you come to the
field?

I prop my phone on the steering wheel and await his
reply.

SENIOR: Be there in 5.

He must be close. Probably at the Hampton across the
street from the campus admin building. I kill the engine
and toss my phone, keys, and wallet into my duffel in the
passenger seat, then grab the straps on my way out of the
car. I pop the trunk and haul out my gear bag, then lug it
over to the main gate.

A perk to being a senior and a team leader is keys to
the kingdom. In this case, the kingdom is the stadium gate
and the practice facilities. I've been using this key a lot,
coming out here in the fall late at night to try to get my
swing back. I haven't come as much since Nikki and I got
together because, well, honestly, I'm happier with her
than I am working out my failures. Maybe I was trying too
hard anyway.

I lean against the wall of honor, where my dad's name
is carved as one of Tiff's greats, along with about fifty
other men, and wait for the familiar rumble of his pickup.
I can't even fathom the gas he blew through on his drives
back and forth over the years. That thing gets about eight
miles to the gallon.

That thought sits in my chest for a moment, and I

work through the math. Not because I want to be shocked at the outrageous expense but because it hits me exactly what he did to be here for me. I'm still computing when he rolls up next to my car. He holds up his hand, then reaches into his truck bed, pulling out the ratty old maroon bag he's carried around with his glove and a few balls since I was in junior high.

I wonder how he knew he'd need that?

He clutches the bag in his right hand while he cradles his mitt to his chest with the other.

"You got the keys?" he asks when he makes it to me.

I push the gate open and he smirks, his eyes masked behind sunglasses. He glances to his right, to the wall, but doesn't mention the fact his name is there. He's not a bragger. He's not much of a talker, really.

I close the gate behind us, then lead him through the clubhouse and out to the side yard where the batting cages are.

"You know we have our own buckets of balls," I say, pointing at his bag. He drops it at his feet and shrugs.

"I like these," he says.

I puff out a short laugh and call him a curmudgeon. He's in his mid-forties, in reality, and in incredible shape. He's a handsome man, I'll admit, and I'm thankful for his genes. But he's also a dog, and I remind myself of that before I get too comfortable with him.

I pull out my bat and lean it against the screen while I wrap my wrists. My dad scoffs, but I simply roll my eyes. He thinks the precautions my generation takes make us soft. I think it'll keep me from crackling with tendonitis and shit the way he snaps and pops around the house.

My dad stretches, rotating his arm a few times. I go through my routine, stretching my quads and flexors, then twisting side to side.

"How's the new stick?" He gestures to my bat. The team all swings the same brand, thanks to deals the school makes. I don't love this one, but I also know better than to blame the bat for my woes. They're all essentially the same.

"She's all right. I don't like the sound," I say. That's something my dad can get behind. We both like the solid click of wood. This thing? It pings. And it's obnoxious.

"Let's give her a ring," he says, moving behind the screen. I nod and take my bat in my hands as I make my way to the plate. I line myself up and twist my back foot into the mat.

"Ready?" my dad asks, holding up one ball, three others clutched in his opposite hand.

I nod.

He winds up and throws it in a little low, but I manage to get the barrel on it and it zings right back at the screen. He flinches, and I snicker.

"Yeah, you always did love telling people about the time you knocked my hat off my head," he says, winding up and throwing another. I hit this one less solid. On the field it would be a pop out. He winces because he knows it too.

"I didn't just knock your hat off. I split your hair." I tap my bat on the plate like I did when I was a kid, then swirl the bat a few times before he readies again.

I read his arm slot and know a curve is coming, so I sit back and drive this one right over his head.

"Woooo weee," he says with a whistle, turning around and pretending to watch the ball sail. It tangled in the net.

"That's over the batter's eye for sure," he says when he turns back around.

I'm not loving how cavalier he is all of a sudden, so I simply nod and dig my foot in again.

He throws another fastball, and while I'm on time, I top it and bounce it back to him. He manages to leap high enough to snag it with his glove, then he pretends to toss it to the invisible first baseman.

"Fuck!" I say, flipping my bat to the ground.

"You're lucky I didn't pay for that," he says, and I know he's joking and making a point at the same time. He doesn't like tantrums. But this isn't about my shitty hit. Or maybe it's *partly* about my shitty hit. Mostly, it's about him.

"This was a bad idea," I say, pulling the Velcro loose from my batting gloves.

I pace the batter's box while my dad stands still, tossing a ball into his own glove at an annoying synchronization. I kick at the ball he pretended to get me out with, and it rolls to the back of the cage.

"Get it all out," he says.

My gaze snaps to him, and my hands form fists at my sides. The leather of my batting gloves stretches around my fingers. I'm not going to hit him. But damn, does a part of me want to.

"How could you?" I finally let out. Hot, angry tears prick at the corners of my eyes.

"There it is," he says, dropping his glove to his feet and crossing his arms over his chest. He's so predictable, even in his posture.

"There I am?" I step toward him, stopping inches from his face.

"Let it out, Mijo."

I growl in his face, my voice echoing around the surrounding concrete.

"You fucking cheat!" I point at his face, and he flinches, but he doesn't move. "How could you do that to her? To us? And with someone I went to school with? Was it going on—"

"No," he butts in, shaking his head. He pulls his glasses from his face and meets my stare. "It absolutely did not start when she was a student. We didn't even talk until she was student teaching."

I laugh out hard.

"Oh, good. That's good. I should give you a prize," I say, my belly burning.

"No, you shouldn't," he says.

I rush him and lunge into his face, our noses inches apart.

"I know!" He takes a step back this time, but he doesn't back down.

"You hurt her," I say, my voice lower as I talk about my mom.

"And I hate that I did."

I laugh again.

"You don't have to believe that. But it's true. I hate that I hurt both of you. I hate what this has done to our relationship. I hate that I'm divorced."

"Well, now you can go run off into the sunset and move in with your girlfriend," I toss out amid jaded cackles.

"Vanessa and I aren't together," he says.

I fall back on my heels for a beat. I didn't know that. And Brayden said they were living together. Of course, Brayden also wants my girl and would say anything to get under my skin.

"Well, I'm not sorry it didn't work out," I grumble.

My dad chuckles, but I'm not amused.

"She's moving to Florida, and I'm getting an apartment near the school. Vanessa and I were not real. We never were. We were a symptom."

"*Pffft!* The fuck does that mean?" He must have gone to a therapy session. Those aren't Alex Senior words.

"It's not an easy thing for me to explain. And I'm not proud of any of it. What happened to me and your mom, that was all my doing. Somewhere along the way, I quit."

Like Mom said. At least they agree on this.

"Well, I'm sorry life didn't work out the way you wanted. You should have gone pro instead and never looked back," I mumble, pulling one of my batting gloves free and tossing it at my gear bag.

"Son," he says, resting a hand on my shoulder. I shirk him off, and he holds up his palms. "I do not regret my decision to stay in Odell, to get married right out of college and start a family, to foster your passion, to get to spend my days on a field throwing a ball to you, none of it. Not for one second. I would have maybe gotten six at bats somewhere in Des Moines and then been done anyway. I'm nowhere close to the talent you are. So don't think any of this, my failures, has anything to do with my choices back then. I was a different man then. A *better* man. And I'm trying really hard to get back to that man. It took fucking up the love of my life to see how far I strayed."

I stare at the ground and soak in his words. They're sobering, and there's so much in them that hits a nerve.

"Was it drugs? Alcohol?" I ask, giving him a sideways glance.

He shakes his head.

"Nothing like that. I think it's just me. I think I got lazy at life. Maybe I got angry somewhere. Small towns can be that way, stifling. It's not an excuse, just the environment. But I got restless, and then I got stupid. And I will regret *that* for as long as I live."

I swallow the harsh lump in my throat. I don't forgive him. I might not ever. But I can live with his admission. I can accept his self-penance. And my God, I can learn from it.

"I told Nik I love her," I let out.

He's quiet for a few seconds, so I glance up and catch his crooked smile.

"Yeah?" he finally says.

I nod. Thinking about her, simply saying her name, feels good. As hard as this moment is, being here with him, just the mere mention of loving her changes it.

"Good. She's meant for you."

"I know," I say, bending down and picking up my bat. I kick a loose ball toward my dad, then walk over to my gear bag and pick my batting glove back up. I put it back on and my dad gathers up the rest of the balls, then drags in the bucket from just outside the net.

"You ready to work?" he asks.

I nod and line myself up at the plate.

"I am."

**19 /
nikki**

MY SEAT IS open as Omar and I walk onto the concourse.

"You chase her away?" my friend says, noticing just after I do.

I shrug, but really? Yeah, I sort of did.

Omar and I settle in and he pulls out his phone, I assume to text Brian. Lacrosse has an away game tomorrow, so they left on the bus early this morning.

"You two seem . . ."

"Serious?" His brow lifts as he types. He clicks send then shifts his gaze to me. He looks a little freaked out. I breathe out a soft laugh.

"Kind of fast, huh?" He flattens his phone on his chest, palm over it in an affectionate way. I think he's in love.

My shoulders hike up briefly.

"Who am I to judge. I'm just the opposite. Kinda slow," I joke.

He leans into me with a laugh, then reads the

incoming text. I peer over and catch the heart Brian sent back but stop short of teasing my friend. It's sweet.

I sink my hands into the front of Alex's hoodie and tuck my chin so I can breathe in the remnants of his shampoo scent. I love this hoodie, and I hope to never ever give it back. But also, he's going to have to wear it periodically so I can get a refill.

The guys are stretching in the outfield, marching in a slow line, lifting one leg at a time then lunging in the other direction and twisting their bodies with their arms out.

"Can they really get a good stretch in like this? It feels more like dance or marching band, the way they're all in unison," Omar says. I cough out a laugh because he's right. It kind of does.

"You would know better than me. I took one biology class. And I barely got a B," I respond.

He elbows me.

"Yeah, because *I* did half of your assignments," he reminds me.

I give him a guilty look and hold out my palms, then turn my attention back to the field. Alex is walking toward me, though a couple hundred feet away on the field. It still feels like he's close. It feels that way every time he moves toward me, looking at me, smiling the way he is. He tips his hat and I hold up my hand.

"You two are adorable, and I mean that in the most sincere, non-grossed-out way," Omar says.

"Thanks," I say, biting my bottom lip.

Brayden is on the mound today, and it's hard not to watch him take his warmups. He makes a show of it, throwing for obscene distances from pole to pole in the outfield. He saw some MLB player do it once when he was young and it became his thing, though really it was the other guy's thing. His thing is copying, but I'll keep that knock to myself.

Glancing to my right, I spot Alex's dad sitting in the same seat as yesterday. He's not like other ballplayers when it comes to superstition. He likes routine, but the "voodoo shit," as he calls it, is all in the head. He's probably right, but I would still feel better if he moved one seat over just to change up the luck.

Alex texted me before the game and said that they had an extremely difficult talk. I didn't ask for details, but I'm sure he'll share them with me later. The parts he did share seem healthy, good. I hope it removes some of the weight from his mind so he can find himself again on the field. I guess today will be a good indicator. I look for signs as he jogs out to the left field grass to throw. It seems there's more zip in his step, but maybe I'm simply hoping.

My eyes follow him everywhere he goes through warmups. And while we stand for the national anthem, I micro-focus on his hands clutched behind his back. He's beautiful, every inch of him a work of discipline. But it's the flaws I'm attracted to most, and maybe because they all have their own stories. Histories I was there for. Origins that involve me.

For example, his right pinky is a little crooked thanks

to a hammer I swung when we tried to build our own treehouse. I think that piece of wood is still precariously nailed to the trunk of the tree in his mom's backyard. That's as far as we got in our construction after I broke his finger.

Then there's the scar across his left knee, where he sliced his skin open on a sharp rock in the lake while we were swimming one summer. And his right eyebrow has the faintest gap. It almost looks intentional, like one of those trendy shaves guys do sometimes. I know better, though. That gap is there because of three stitches after Alex took a fist from a boy twice his size in fifth grade. That boy, Colton Wagner, tried to look up my skirt during school choir. Alex left a few marks of his own on Colton.

All of these slight imperfections build an amazing man, and I love him so much that sometimes my heart feels too full.

My phone buzzes as I sink down into my seat, ready for the first pitch. I read the short text, a confirmation for my CT scan in two days, and then the number to set up a consultation with a surgeon. Alex's talk with his dad was hard, and I promised I'd meet him—hard thing for hard thing. But this feels *too* hard. Every time I truly think about the possibilities and the potential outcomes, I get a little queasy.

I put my phone away before that happens now and prop my feet up on the seat in front of me, my right foot finding its favorite nook. I smirk, and Omar catches me.

"What's that look for?"

I wiggle my foot along the loose armrest.

"There are many reasons I love this seat. I'm just glad to have it back."

I pull Alex's hood up over my head and hold on to the strings to give myself something to fidget with, and Brayden slings the first pitch in for a strike.

"He is good," Omar comments.

"And he knows it," I add.

I filled my friend in on almost everything. He was most impressed that Alex chucked him through a screen door. I don't think Omar really understands construction and the concept of flimsy.

But he is right—Brayden is good at one thing. He strikes out the side in eleven pitches, and his team rushes off the field behind him, every player patting him on the back as they pass by. Except Alex, who makes a point to praise the catcher instead.

Alex is back at short today, which eases my anxious insides on his behalf. But he's batting eighth. It's not where he should be, but I know he'll get himself back to that lead-off spot or the two-hole. I just hope his streak starts today. I hope his time in the cage with his dad, while difficult, delivers the magic he always swore by growing up.

Tiff manages to score one run in the first, but Brayden gives up a solo shot to right in the second. We're playing Commonwealth, a smaller Division One school with a lot of money. They suck at football, but they've always had great baseball squads. I think these have been some of my favorite games to watch over the years.

The pitcher slinging for them today is easily hitting a hundred on his fastball. Alex is convinced that parents are juicing up their kids young to max out their muscles early so they can throw so fast. I'm shitty at science, but I'm pretty sure it doesn't work that way. I can't imagine guys like this can keep that sort of thing up for years. It has to tear up their arms. The ball hits the catcher's mitt with a snap just as I have the thought.

Alex is up third this inning, and when the two hitters before him fly out to the centerfielder, I grow tense.

"Relax," Omar says, squeezing my denim-covered knee. I grit my teeth because he's trying to be a good friend, but I hate being told to relax. I don't think I could right now for a million dollar bill, if that's even a thing.

I tuck my hands under my thighs and lock in on my heart as Alex holds his bat up like a lightsaber and takes a deep breath as he stares at it. His shoulders fall on his exhale, and he steps into the box. I glance at Senior, who is sitting back, hands over his chest, sunglasses down. Everything is normal.

Okay. Come on, Alex.

The first pitch rips by him and he takes it, called for a strike.

"Boo! You're blind," Omar shouts, cupping his mouth.

It was a pretty solid pitch but I love how supportive he's being of Alex. My chest tightens and I shift my legs, driving my hands under my weight more.

Alex nods, his body loose. It's a different him from the one I've seen take strikes over the last several months. As he sets up in the box again, all those little nuances that have always added up to something spectacular click into place. His body lowers another tick, his thighs flexing and bat poised just over his shoulder. The tiny ticks in his wrist count down the milliseconds, and my heart syncs up with them.

The young punk on the mound gasses in another fastball, probably figuring that Alex can't keep up, but he is wrong. Alex puts a swing on the ball that launches it down the left field line, barely fair, and it lands in the corner where the wall juts out in an odd shape, which makes life miserable for anyone playing left field out there.

Alex slides into second easily and starts clapping hard before he even stands up.

"Wooo! Let's go, baby!" he shouts, his team on the dugout wall, rowdy as hell.

Somewhere along the way, I got to my feet. I don't even remember standing. I've pushed his hoodie back and my hands are on my head. His gaze shifts to me, and I lift my hands up and scream as loud as I fucking can. He holds his up, and basically, air high-fives me. Or maybe it's tens me. I don't know, but we celebrate this together. The seal is fucking broken. The lid is off. Alex Mendoza? He's back!

I hug Omar to my left, shaking him, and he laughs at my exuberance. We plop back into our seats and I inhale the deepest breath I've taken in weeks. Months.

"I haven't seen you this excited since you dragged me to see the Phantom Aunt show in that underground venue in November," Omar says.

I shake my head.

"That's because I haven't been!"

I glance to my right and lean forward a tick to get Senior's attention, but he hasn't moved from his spot. His arms still crossed over his chest, his eyes seem focused on his son, as if he's studying. He is, however, smiling. That is unmistakable. It's the one trait that marks them both like beams of light.

Alex makes it home by stealing third and getting knocked in off a single. The game stays tied all the way into the ninth until Brayden is pulled, and a sophomore reliever comes in and gives up a three-run homer that was barely fair.

The shot is deflating, but for the first time in a while, I feel the charge of optimism in my chest. I do the math as our first batter gets on. A walk follows, then Edwin sends a line drive over the third baseman that loads the bases. Yesterday, I would be praying for someone else to take the wheel right now, for anyone but Alex to do the work. But now? I want these next two fools to strike out so the love of my life can win the fucking game.

The first hitter cracks the first pitch right back to the pitcher for a quick out, and I clutch the front of Alex's hood in my fist and hold it against my heart. It's Cole, and I feel guilty rooting against him, so I send up a silent prayer that he's allowed to tie the game if need be. He just can't win it.

"Please, please, please," I mutter softly, over and over, as I rock where I stand. Omar slips his arm through mine and rocks with me.

Cole strikes out and there's an audible, crushing *aww* from the surprisingly decent crowd of a few hundred. I, however, smile. Because this is how I planned it. This was my instant play-by-play that I sent up to heaven seconds ago. I'm sure it was Senior's too.

As Alex steps up to the plate, everyone in the stadium gets to their feet. I glance to my right, and Senior is on his too, though his arms are still crossed over his chest and his shades are still snug on his face.

Alex digs in, and I find myself taking a deep breath. I see him exhale when his shoulders drop. The first pitch is low for a ball and the crowd roars.

"Okay, that's good. He can walk too. Walk scores a run," Omar chants.

I shake my head.

"Uh uh," I say. "He's got this."

The next pitch comes in for a strike, a fastball that Alex swings through and fouls into the dugout like a bullet.

"Or he can walk," Omar says, only half joking. For wanting to be a trauma nurse, he's not great at stress.

"Nope," I say, holding out for my wish to come through.

Alex nods, his eyes studying his hands as they stretch around the grip. He pushes the top of his helmet down snug, an anxious habit he used to do in high school, and my mouth curves into a grin.

"He's back," I say.

The Commonwealth pitcher slows down his approach, and he stares at the runner on third for an extra second or two before slinging the ball home, a slow curve that even I see coming. Alex's weight shifts, his body coiling and his front foot lifting for a high kick. It's the sound that clinches it. That perfect, crisp pop of the leather meeting its match. Alex doesn't run. He flips his bat back and strolls, nodding as he watches the ball sail over the scoreboard and into the maintenance lot.

"Yeah, baby!" I scream, my hands up as I jump up and down.

Alex makes the slow trot to first, his fist pumping as his team pours out of the dugout and rushes to home plate. Every run that comes in earns a "boom!" from the squad, but it's Alex's trip down the third base line that causes a frenzy throughout the stadium. By the time he stomps on home, he's swallowed up by his team, buried under bodies then quickly hoisted on shoulders and rushed to the middle of the infield.

I cup my mouth, my massive grin sticking out on either side of my hand.

"That was fucking amazing," Omar says, showing me his phone. I didn't even know he was recording.

"Send that to me!" I clutch at his arm.

"Nik, I'm sending that to *everybody!* This puppy is going viral."

I ditch my friend while he types on his phone to keep his word and rush down to the gate next to the Tiff dugout. My nervous hands flounder around the latch, and I'm about to climb my ass over the backstop to get to Alex when a woman I recognize as Cole's mom steps forward and helps me out.

"Thanks," I say through a toothy grin. She laughs and ushers me through, shouting, "Go celebrate!"

Alex is still engulfed by his teammates, a few of them drenching him in the team Gatorade while others pour on buckets of gum and seeds. He laughs through the rain of junk, then our eyes meet and he literally shoves his friends out of the way to rush toward me.

I leap at him, wrapping my legs around him and clutching his face as our mouths crash. I kiss him hard and boastfully as he holds me tight, one hand under my body and the other in my hair, holding my head to his. We smile through it but never let up as he turns us slowly, messing up the dirt on the mound while he claims my mouth as his trophy—me as his prize.

When he finally sets my feet back down on the dirt, I leave my arms locked around him, my fingers stretching to hook together under his opposite arm as I remain glued to his side while people assail him with shoulder smacks and compliments. I won't let go through the madness, just like I won't let go through the quiet. I'm here for him. Always.

"You see my dad?" Alex asks, his lips at my ear.

I nod and shift my gaze over to the area where he was

sitting. His seat is now empty. The man is gone. But he was here. He was here through it all.

"He must have left after your home run," I say.

"He did," Alex says, but it isn't a disappointed response at all. "He saw the important part. And we've talked enough for today."

I nod, then pull up to kiss him again, my palm flattening on his cheek.

I wrap my hands around his bicep and wait with him while he talks to the local and student reporters now out on the field. I look out toward the parking lot where the familiar lifted pickup is pulling onto the main road, and I smile.

That fucker didn't uncross his arms a single time. *Not superstitious my ass!*

**20 /
alex**

NIKKI'S KNEE knocks into mine at a regular pace. I don't dare tell her to relax because, one, she hates that, and two, she has every right to let out her nerves. This is terrifying for her.

"I'm so hungry," she whines, the clipboard on her thighs vibrating with her constant movement. I bite my tongue and don't tell her to stop wasting calories fidgeting. Now is not the time.

"I've got a great lunch spot for us," I say, resting my hand on her knee. I subtly slow the movement, but she gives me side eyes.

"Sorry," I whisper, squeezing once then pulling my hand away.

"I don't have time for lunch," she says.

I chuckle.

"Don't pretend you don't want to miss accounting. I'll help you with your assignment." Her head swivels, and she hits me with a short-lived but honest grin. It slips back to the focused straight line, but it's still in there.

Nikki had to fast for this appointment. She's not great at being *hangry,* as we call it. That's the other reason I'm doing my best not to poke the bear.

I think she's really going to like this place I found for lunch. This location comes with an ulterior motive, but a good one. I remember eating there with my parents once when they came up for the weekend to visit. It was the *before* time, when our family unit was cohesive and we all got along, for the most part. There was this woman who played guitar in the corner, singer-songwriter type music. She was really talented, but she was also legally deaf. My mom has no problem talking to strangers, and she basically pulled the girl's life story out of her. It stuck with me because of her perseverance, having lost most of her hearing after a long battle with meningitis in high school. I called ahead to see if she was still there, and with some luck, she happens to be today.

"Miss Thomas?" Nikki looks at me first, a flash of panic in her eyes. I think if I weren't here she might sit here silent and wait for them to go searching for her so she can slip out unnoticed and go home.

"I'm right here," I assure her. If I could get in that scan with her, I would.

"Okay," she says.

"Yes," she utters, standing and holding the clipboard flat against her legs, kicking it with her thighs as she marches forward like a stubborn, nervous grade-schooler.

"Hi, Nikki. I'm Jasmine," the technician says, and Nikki flashes me a quick smile to see if I caught that her name is the same as Nikki's middle.

I give her a thumbs up.

All good signs.

When she disappears behind the door, I lean forward and look through the game film I had our hitting coach send me from our last series. I'm improving, and my average is finally starting to look like me again. But something still feels off, so I want to study my swings.

I play the clips a few times, slowing them down and zooming in to check my rotation, my hips and shoulders all seemingly lined up right. I memorized Nikki's routine for this scan based on the paperwork so I keep checking the time to imagine the steps she's at. The actual scan itself is quick, but the contrast solution administration takes some time. Nikki doesn't love needles, so I imagine the IV process was somewhat challenging for all.

She should be well into that, though. I just hope she doesn't vomit from anxiety or the solution. I read some people do. And Nikki sure does like a good cookie-tossing session. It's half the reason she stopped drinking a lot at parties our freshman year. Though a part of me likes to think she blames her intoxication for her poor judgment in ever saying yes to Brayden.

I run through my video clips one more time, putting off what my inner voice suggested I do this morning—send them to my dad.

I'm so fucking conflicted over him. I can't really stand

being in the same room with him, but there's also a part of me that wants to get over that. I think my mom would prefer I don't hold a lifelong grudge. That's her way, though. Marie Mendoza is an optimist, the world rose-colored through her eyes, her son perfect, her ex-husband flawed but trying. I aspire to find more of her in my fabric. I hope it's there. But I've come around to the idea that a lot of my father is. And if his flaws are part of me too, at least I'm aware of them. Giving up on making Nikki happy simply isn't an option.

After another twenty minutes, I relent and type out a message, sending my father the video links and asking for his input. I know he'll see what I'm missing. He always says that sometimes we look for things to use as a crutch. Maybe that's what's happening here. And if that's the case, he'll tell me—in all his harsh and direct glory. It's baseball, not intimacy. Perhaps that's why my father has always been better at speaking its language.

He responds a few minutes after my text.

> SENIOR: Are you coming to Odell anytime soon?

I sigh and read his words a few times, knowing what he means. He's found something. And he'd like to help me fix it. A part of me would like that too.

> ME: Did not plan on it.

His response comes fast.

SENIOR: I'll drive up Friday.

I swallow but also realize that he has my schedule memorized. He knows that Friday is an off-day for us. We have a doubleheader Saturday and a game Sunday instead. If Friday goes well, maybe I'll invite him to stay for the games. Or maybe I won't, and he'll just invite his damn self like he did last time.

I chuckle quietly.

ME: K

No *I love you* or friendly banter. It's all business for now. Maybe in a few months we can add in some chatter about playoffs and other teams. And if the draft goes well, maybe . . . *maybe* . . . I'll ask him to be a part of the signing.

He's already one up on me for son-to-father favors as it is. Fucker drove behind the field after my grand slam and nabbed the ball. Sent me a pic of it later that night. Said he's keeping it on his desk at work.

I'm not sure I would have given it to him if I had the option, but part of me is also glad he has it. It feels nice to know he's proud. One more thing my mom was right about.

"Sir?"

I pop my head up and shove my phone into my back pocket to meet the eyes of the assistant who led Nikki back for her scan. My pulse picks up with worry.

"Yes." I scramble to my feet.

She smiles softly, probably amused at how my panic matches the patient's, but it puts me at ease.

"She's getting dressed. She was a little anxious, and she's afraid she might faint, so she asked if you could come back and help her out to the car."

"Of course." I follow her back to the dressing room area. I wait with her outside the door while my eyes focus on the shadows moving around the space at the bottom of the doorway. Nikki's hopping, trying to push her foot into her shoe, so I knock softly.

"Hey, Nik? You need a hand?"

The door clicks and inches open.

"Please," she says.

"May I?" I ask the technician.

She chuckles.

"That's up to her."

I nod and step inside as Niki slumps back into the chair. She doesn't faint, but she sure is sweating, and her face is practically gray.

I pick her shoe up off the floor and hold out my other hand.

"Gimme," I say, and she lifts her leg, propping her heel in my palm.

I work her shoe on, then snag the other one from the floor and do the same. Once she's fully dressed and has had a minute to regulate her breathing, I hoist her up in my arms. She doesn't even protest that I'm carrying her through the lobby, which means as stubborn as she can be, she's that much more freaked out by this experience.

"I hope you're still up for lunch," I say as I lean over to help her buckle in. Her hand finds my chin, nudging me to look her in the eyes.

"I could be dead and I would still be up for lunch," she jokes.

I laugh, then close the small gap between our mouths to kiss her.

"All right then."

Not wanting to send her into a new round of panic, I keep my ulterior motive to myself on our drive into the historic downtown. I luck out with a spot right by the door, but Nikki seems solid enough on her feet now to get up to the curb on her own. Her arm is wrapped with a bright green bandage from the IV, and there's a small stain in the center which means she probably bled a little bit. She's not great with blood.

Wow, when we have kids one day, I'm going to do a lot of the gross stuff.

I let that thought simmer in my chest, keeping it to myself as we enter the café. Kids with Nik. Now that I'm manifesting the idea, it feels so probable.

"This place is nice," she says, taking in the open dining room that leads right out onto a patio and a grassy seating area in the back.

"My mom loves this place," I say.

"Kind of jealous she never brought me here when she took us both out," Nikki says. We both follow the hostess, who gives me a wink, having read my notes when I called ahead. She puts us at a table just inside the main dining space and to the side of the small platform where a guitar rests on a stool.

"There's music?" Nikki brightens.

I nod with a smile.

I scan the restaurant, spotting the woman I want her to meet at the other end of the bar. She's drinking water, probably on her break. I didn't go so far as to call her ahead of time too, but I remember her being kind enough that if I can urge Nikki to talk with her, she'll be happy to.

We order drinks, Nikki splurging with a sugary smoothie type thing. I encourage her to also guzzle down some water, but she's probably had plenty of that. Water is the *only* thing she's had for twenty-four hours. And lots of it. Apparently, you need to have your insides float for a proper CT scan.

"Hi, I'm Annabeth," the woman says softly through the mic.

Nikki puts down her glass and folds her hands together as she leans onto the table, her eyes immediately noticing the cochlear implants on her ears. Her gaze shifts to me, and I suck my mouth into a guilty, straight line.

Her head falls to the side a touch, having caught on.

"Trust me," I say, and she takes a deep breath through her nose and gives me a tepid nod.

"This one's called 'Love, Actually,' and no, not after the movie." The few people in the restaurant with us titter, and when I glance at Nikki, she's smiling at the joke.

Annabeth works her hands up the guitar, her eyes focused intently on every touch, her chin tucked in as she studies herself. I remember her telling us that she likes to see the music work. It sets her brain up to sing confidently, knowing that part is right.

And her playing is beautiful. Her touch goes from soft to intentional, the shift easy and natural. I don't really know shit about music other than what I like, but I'd say she's definitely mastered the nuances.

When she leans into the mic and begins to sing, Nikki sits back, letting her folded hands fall into her lap. Her lips part, and for a long while she doesn't blink. She simply listens and watches. I'm not sure what she hears because I don't really understand what she's missing now. The doctor did tell her that she may have been missing the midrange for years, which means she's already learned how to maneuver around the loss. But Nikki doesn't believe that's the case. She would know best.

Annabeth finishes, and Nikki claps softly, her eyes shifting to me for a second, long enough to soften and show that she's giving in.

"Yeah?" I say.

She nods.

"This was a good plan, Alex Mendoza." She leans into the corner of the table, and I meet her halfway for a kiss as our waiter drops off our lunch.

Nikki devours the burger in minutes, beating me, and at one point I notice Annabeth smirk at seeing the petite girl out eat the muscle man. We order dessert, cheesecake, because my girlfriend is obsessed with the stuff, just as

Annabeth announces another break. I nod to Nikki, urging her to introduce herself.

She breathes out some stress, then leans into the table, making eye contact with the musician.

"Excuse me, but could I . . . can I ask you something?" Nikki's gaze drifts to me for a second.

"I've seen you play before. I came here with my mom," I insert, filling the silence and setting Nikki at ease. She doesn't want to be the only one talking. I can tell.

"Aww, thank you for coming again. And sure. What can I answer?" Annabeth pulls a chair from our table and takes a seat while my girlfriend kneads her hands together on top of the table. It catches Annabeth's eye, and I think maybe she has a hunch what has Nikki's tongue tied.

"It's the implant, right?" She reaches up her right hand and runs her fingertip along the edge.

"Yeah, and sort of the whole thing. How do you— You sing so well. And you play . . ."

Annabeth chuckles.

"I wasn't always deaf. In high school, I got really sick with meningitis. I was a pretty big music nerd. Only member of the guitar club," she says, raising her hand.

Nikki's hands part and flatten on the table, her shoulders relaxing as she lets out a soft laugh.

"I was the only girl in the AV Club," she says, holding up her hand. Annabeth gives her five, and I sit back in wonder as the two women form an instant bond.

We spend an hour at the café, waiting through Annabeth's final set so Nikki can continue learning how she made the decision to get the implants and when. How it changed her practice, what she hears and feels. How her body adjusted, and her mind. And they talk about the grief and depression, the part that lingers in the shadow and, I know, eats at Nikki's soul.

I pay the bill as Nikki and Annabeth exchange numbers, and we walk our new friend out to her Volkswagen. I carry her amp, tucking it in the tight back seat. These cars are stupid. Quirky, but stupid. I keep that to myself.

They hug, Nikki promising to come to her first solo show at the Rebel House next week. I'd usually send Omar with her to something like this. But this time? I think I want to come along. In fact, I might not send Omar in my place for anything ever again if I can help it.

Because I'm never going anywhere.

july, after graduation

MY HOUSE IS a buzz of activity with family and friends claiming every seat and square foot of standing room with a view of the television. Nikki pushes herself into the non-existent free space on our family couch, her right leg slung over my left just to fit. She knows better than to try to move my mom from my right side, and my dad has the back of the sofa on lockdown. I don't think his hands have left the cushion in twenty minutes as he leans over, hands braced about five feet apart and gripping like he's trying to push a Cadillac up a hill. His back is going to suffer for this, the way he's leaning, lunging.

"You can see the same thing if you don't hover," my mom says.

"I know," he grumbles.

I chuckle as I make eyes at Nikki. We've noticed that

for a man who claims baseball superstitions are "a bunch of hooey," he sure does have a lot of interesting habits he refuses to break when something is going well.

Having my entire family together for the draft was only a dream a few months ago. My immediate family seemed so broken, and my odds of being drafted at all felt pretty fucking slim.

But we have come a long way, my mom maybe the most, though she would argue that my all-star nod and slugging awards to end my season probably takes the cake. It's nothing compared to her personal growth, though.

I didn't know at the time, but while she was finalizing the divorce, she was also going back to school for her master's degree online. It's one of those things she left hanging and unfinished, and when my dad let her down, she decided to quit letting herself down, too.

It will take her about a year to complete, but then she wants to look into getting a job at Tiff. Of course, that probably means that Nikki's parents will be selling their place and moving west a couple hours as well. Marie and Julianne haven't been more than a mile apart since they were born in separate hospitals on different days—barely different days. Kinda like me and Nik.

As for my dad, he'll never leave Odell. The high school team had a rough year, probably because he kept cutting practices short and leaving his assistants in charge so he could drive to Tiff and watch me. *From the same seat every time.*

I was glad he was there. I never invited him officially. And he never asked. It's something we both sort of let happen, and eventually, before the season was up, he stuck around to shake my hand after a game.

We silently built a new off-day routine too. It would start with a text from me asking if he was around. And usually about ten minutes later he'd send an ETA. We'd meet at the cages at the stadium, slipping in and out without fanfare, without anyone but Coach, who caught us once, knowing what we were up to.

It was working. I was soaring. And my dad, he was making amends about the only way he knows how.

Our relationship is still stunted, and maybe it will always be like this. But I'd like to have faith in myself that sometime down the road, I'll forgive him. My mom has, though she still doesn't like him hovering over her behind the couch.

"*¡Sientante!*" she finally snaps, pointing to the open chair next to the TV.

Senior grumbles and I can feel the tension grow between them. Okay, so things aren't quite perfect.

"Beat you with my *chancla*," my mom mutters under her breath. She's always threatening to smack us with her flip-flop. She'd be so proud of the way Nikki threw her shoes at me a while back.

"Let him stand there. He's superstitious," I say to my mom. Nikki snorts a laugh then cups her mouth, blushing and guilty.

"I am not," my dad grumbles. He sure as shit doesn't move, though, and that amuses all of us.

"You so are, Alex," my mom says, looking up from her spot, staring at his chin while he holds his head still, eyes on the TV, never once acknowledging her words. In a way, his silence is acquiescing that she's right. Or maybe that's how I take it. I think it's how she does as she turns back around and purses her lips into a smug little triumph that only I seem to notice.

"Okay, you should get a call in about five," my uncle Joe says. He's been helping with all of the craziness leading up to the draft. My mom's brother is a contract lawyer, and since I can't have an official agent, he's the next best thing to make sure I do all of this by the book.

"You ready?" Nikki says, laying an open palm on my thigh. I cover her hand with mine and thread our fingers together, bringing her hand to my mouth.

"Not at all," I laugh out.

The house is beginning to fill with the rich flavors my abuela and Nikki's mom have been cooking in the kitchen. Two families' worth of hungry people are crammed into this tiny-ass house. Once I get this announcement done, there's going to be a herd headed into that kitchen. I hope they're prepared.

"Hey! Look who made it," Nikki's dad, Andrew, announces.

"Papa!" Nikki flies to entry, leaving me in the dust so she can wrap her arms around her father. I'm a little jealous that she can do that, but not so much that I would ever want to diminish it for her. Plus, I'd really like to call him Dad someday.

"Alex," he says, meeting my gaze as his daughter skips back to her seat, half on me, which feels odd under his stare.

"Thank you for making it in time, Andy." I've always called him that, though now that I'm sleeping with his daughter, I feel like maybe I should start using Sir. I think that would stand out more, though, and then we'd likely both be thinking about why I'm saying it. And then *he* would think about me and what I'm doing to his little girl. And then . . . well, then I'd be dead, so that's the end of that.

"I brought you a little something," he says, reaching over my girl cousins who have not put their phones down since they plopped their asses on the coffee table in front of me and Mom.

I lean forward to take an envelope from him and slip out the small card inside.

"Holy crap, how did you?" It's a baseball card. *My* baseball card, though not authentic. My image, clearly Photoshopped into the right uniform, is standing in the middle of Wrigley Field.

"You better not have jinxed this, Andy," my dad grumbles.

I drop my head in laughter, my dad oblivious to the fact he just proved our point from earlier. *Superstitious as fuck!*

Nikki takes the card from me, running her finger fondly over my image.

"That's pretty cool," I say, then glance to her dad. "Thanks for that."

He nods.

And then my phone buzzes in my lap.

"Shit!" I wave my hands and everyone hushes. My dad leans over enough to practically take the call with me, and I let him.

"Hello?" I'm too tongue-tied to say anything else, and it's not like this is a spam call. I know the number.

"Hey, Alex. This is John Westhover with the Chicago Cubs. I'm calling to officially offer you a spot in our system in the third round of this year's draft. What do you say?"

My heart wants to explode in my chest. My arm flies around Nikki, and I hold her close to me, squeezing her so hard I'm sure she can barely breathe.

"Yes, sir. Yes, I'd be honored," I say, my uncle pulling out the hat he's been waiting to reveal. He plops it on my head and I push it down, my body shaking with happiness while the man on the other line walks me through all of the terms I was expecting. There will be a formal signing soon, and my uncle will be there for that, too. But for now, I end the call with about seven thank yous, then toss my phone in the air, not caring who it hits.

My dad grabs my shoulders, squeezing them once, and I turn to face him and give him a hug. I feel his body quake under my embrace, and the moment is just as hard for me. But it's also amazing. And I needed it. I needed him. Even when I didn't want to.

I kiss Nikki next, then turn to hold my mom, who is not usually a crier but is one today.

"You're going to have to start coming to games," I tease her. She playfully shoves at my chest, then presses her hands to my cheeks as she stares into my eyes, nodding.

I shake about a million hands, and relatives I haven't seen since the last family wedding pile on me, knocking my new hat off and messing up my hair. I basically look like I've been run over by the time Nikki's mom shouts, "Food is ready!"

Nikki and I hang back, letting everyone rush into the tight space. It gives us a short moment alone. The end of the year was so chaotic with the season getting hot and then playoffs; quiet time has been hard to come by for the two of us. And when we're alone together at night, it's rather impossible to keep our fucking hands to ourselves. Whoever said athletes shouldn't fuck before gameday is a moron. There's no science to the theory that having sex diminishes performance in the sport, at least not for me. And Nikki and I have tested that theory thoroughly, perhaps once in the clubhouse several hours before a game.

Okay. Twice.

Nik got her formal diagnosis a few weeks after her scan. And she's met with three different surgeons about options. I went with her to the first two. Annabeth joined her for the third. And while it took some time for her to navigate her worst fears, I think arming herself with information and forming a close friendship with Annabeth has helped her feel secure in her decision. She's going to monitor the tumor, and if her hearing gets any worse, she'll consider surgery or radiation.

Her audio mixing hasn't seemed to suffer at all, at least as far as I can tell. Annabeth seems to think she's a wizard, too, having paid her a pretty hefty sum as a freelance sound artist to help her put together her first album. They're finishing it up this summer. Nikki thinks it's going to be huge. I kind of think so too.

Of course, I also think Nikki is going to be huge in the industry. Annabeth might be a newbie on the scene, but she's garnered some hype. And last week, a pretty big name down in Houston called and invited Nikki out to chat and help with a recording as a test. She swore me to secrecy; apparently there's an NDA. But let's just say the guy likes tattoos on his face.

Someone knocks over one of my abuela's bowls in the kitchen, and a round of *ooooooohs* emanates from the crowded space while the tiny woman in her late sixties threatens to swat someone with her spoon.

They're all going to crowd back in here soon, so I take this time and kiss my girl without an audience.

"This is weird, huh?" she says, nuzzling her nose against mine after our lips part.

I let my head fall back with a short laugh, but right it quickly, then look her in the eyes while we stand amid the mess my family and hers left in the living room. I cup her face with my hands, my thumbs sweeping her hair from her eyes while she holds onto my elbows.

I shake my head, then let it fall against hers as I close my eyes, my cheeks aching from the smile I don't think I will ever be able to shake.

"No, Nik. It isn't weird at all. It's perfect."

epilogue

2 Years Later

nikki

"DRUGS ARE GOOD," I mumble.

I just woke up from surgery. At least, I *think* I just woke up from surgery. Maybe I've been awake for a while. Maybe . . . *oh!* What if I haven't even *had* surgery yet!

"All of this is out loud, Nik. All of it," Alex says.

I roll my head to the side and meet all four of his eyes.

"You're pretty," I slur.

He chuckles and leans over me. His head is enormous. His mouth is coming at me so I better make fish lips. I pucker and feel his soft lips mush against mine.

"You kiss good," I say.

He pulls back, and now he has two eyes. At least it isn't three.

"I kiss good. Drugs are good. Everything is good, isn't it, Nik? We can *all* hear you," he says.

Of course they can hear me. Duh. I'm talking. I roll my

head more, my eyes landing on his crotch, and I reach for it.

"Your cock is good," I say.

"Ohhhhhh kay." He backs up.

"What? I like it. I. Like. Cock!"

"Nicole Jasmine!" My mom's voice rings out, and I sober up a touch. But I still laugh.

"Mama," I say, rolling my head the other way.

She takes my hand, and I think she's shaking her head, muttering something about me being pregnant before Alex puts a ring on my finger. That won't happen. Because *I'm* going to propose. I dreamt it while I was under. Maybe I'm still dreaming it.

I lift my hand and flex my fingers above my face, the pic line dragging along behind.

"Wee ooo," I say, swirling my hand around like a roller-coaster.

"Okay, maybe let's . . . can we give her a minute?" Alex seems to be urging people out of the room. I wonder who else is here. I sure hope a doctor is here.

Oh. White coat! That's the doctor. Good.

"Hi, Nikki. It's Dr. Singh. You did great. It's going to take a few more minutes for you to fully wake up, but I want you to know that you did perfect. In a few months we'll test your hearing again, and I have a really good feeling that you'll be close to one hundred percent."

I take his hand and squeeze it, my mind coming to enough to recognize the good news.

"Thank you," I say, my voice sounding a little less

cartoon-like to myself. It's still very much inside my head, though. Probably from post-op.

"No swimming," I say to him, pointing.

He chuckles, then looks to Alex. He's wearing one of his MLB shirts. He got called up last month and he looks so good in Cubbie blue. We love it in Chicago. The winter is like Iowa, but the spring and summer feel more alive. Maybe there are just more people.

I moved here with Alex when he got called up. We were in Iowa City for a while before that. It's been two years, and this life we've started together feels exactly as I imagined it would.

I found studio space last month and got approved for my first business loan. I can't ever leave Alex now because we both know I don't know shit about accounting. But I do know music. And after Annabeth's debut blew up, work started pouring in. I never had to apprentice. And this studio space is long overdue.

Alex and the doctor talk for a few minutes, then shake hands before my love comes back to stand at my side. I decided to give the surgery a try after a full year of intense research. The team at the University of Chicago Medical Center is renowned. And after talking with Dr. Singh, I knew I was ready.

"I might be drunk," I say to Alex now that we're alone. Not as drunk as I just was. The sobering is happening fast.

"You are definitely high. But you're also beautiful." He sits on the edge of the bed and leans down to kiss my head. I trap him with a palm to his chin and urge his lips to mine for a real kiss. I'm pretty sure I goofed the first one.

I take in a deep breath, a little soreness settling in my ear.

"Ooooo!" I wince.

"Yeah, you'll get more of the good stuff soon. And then it's gonna be a rough few days at home. But he says it should heal pretty fast." Alex's eyes are so reassuring. It hits me now how awful I must look to him.

"Ugh, I cannot be very pretty right now. You said beautiful, you liar," I say, feeling the nest on top of my head.

He runs his fingers through it as best he can and chuckles.

"No, still beautiful. Knots and all."

I squint my eyes.

"So, I was planning on doing this a whole different way. And a few days from now. But since you went ahead and drunkenly proposed to me a few minutes ago in front of your mom, and in front of Omar and Brian, I figure maybe I should scrap the plans." Alex rests a small yellow box on my chest.

"No!" I lift up but quickly lay back down. "Ooooof, can't do that."

Alex chuckles and opens the box for me, pulling out the perfect platinum ring, a modest diamond center and two pink stones on either side.

"Oh, my God!" I cry out. My eyes flash to his, and I can feel the tears already streaking my cheeks.

"This is a good cry. It doesn't count!" I sniffle, and he

takes care of the tears for me, swiping them away with his thumb.

"So that's a yes?" he asks.

I nod as best I can but utter, "Yes" loudly. He slips the ring on my finger and leans in to kiss me deeper. The chatter outside my door tells me that my visitors were probably listening to this whole thing. Of course, *oh shit . . . did I really propose?*

I cover my face when he sits up and look at him through my fingers.

"Did I really propose in front of my mom?" Oh, my God, she's probably out there thinking shotgun wedding because her baby girl is pregnant!

Alex laughs and nods.

"You did. But you always did have to be first."

I let the embarrassment drift away, instead owning my doped-up behavior.

"Just like I loved you first."

He leans in and gives me another soft, chaste kiss, then peels back with a dimple and that heart-fluttering wink.

"Sure, you did."

THE END

The Varsity Series

Begin Your Binge with Varsity Heartbreaker

Lucas Fuller is a lot of things.
He's the boy next door.
He's the first crush I ever had.
He was my first kiss.
He's also the only person who has ever broken my heart.
For two years, I've wondered what happened to the us I used to know.
We were best friends, and then suddenly…we weren't.
I tried to run away from it. I even changed schools just to make the hurt disappear.
But no matter how hard I tried to not think about Lucas, I just couldn't stay away from the high school quarterback with perfect blue eyes and so many secrets.
I'm back. We're seniors now. We've grown—all of us. And Lucas Fuller might be different, but I'm different too.

This is my time to take risks, to experience life and to fall in love for real.

I want Lucas Fuller to be a part of my story, but I know for that to happen, I need to know the truth about our past.

acknowledgments

Writing this part is always bittersweet when I come to the end of a series. And this series—oooof! I had so much fun, and I cannot thank you all enough for taking the ride with me. I wanted to jump feet first into my kind of sports romance and turn the heat up a bit. Okay, *quite* a bit. This series is about love, escapism, connections, friendships, family and what it really means to win. I, for one, feel that I have won a lot by getting to make up stories for a living. So thanks.

Huge shout out to my team for supporting me through this book and the series, starting with Brenda Letendre, my angel of an editor, and Autumn with Wordsmith. I love you both so much and am so lucky to have you behind me, believing in me, and putting me in the right kind of shape.

Forever thanks to my mom, who is my backbone in all ways; my boys, who are my heart; and my incredible friends, who never hesitate to answer my strange texts at odd hours to fact check random pieces of information that I decide *need* to be in my story. Big hugs and thanks to Laura Rodriguez for helping me make sure I nailed exactly what it was her mom would yell at her and her brother when we all got to be a little too much.

While this series is done, you know me . . . I will never say never to returning. I really liked writing characters who were Tiff Tuff. So maybe we will get another class of athletes down the road. For now, I have a lot of strange and wonderful ideas ready to fly from my brain. Let's hope my fingers can keep up.

XO
   Ginger

also by ginger scott

Final Score Series

The Tomboy & The Captain

The Wallflower & The Running Back

The Best Friend & The Short Stop

The Boys of Welles

Loner

Rebel

Habit

The Fuel Series

Shift

Wreck

Burn

The Varsity Series

Varsity Heartbreaker

Varsity Tiebreaker

Varsity Rule breaker

Varsity Captain

The Waiting Series

Waiting on the Sidelines

Going Long

The Hail Mary

Like Us Duet

A Boy Like You

A Girl Like Me

The Falling Series

This Is Falling

You And Everything After

The Girl I Was Before

In Your Dreams

The Harper Boys

Wild Reckless

Wicked Restless

Standalone Reads

The Moon and Back

Southpaw

Candy Colored Sky

Cowboy Villain Damsel Duel

Drummer Girl

BRED

The Hard Count

Memphis

Hold My Breath

Blindness

How We Deal With Gravity

about the author

Ginger Scott is a *USA Today, Wall Street Journal* and Amazon-bestselling author from Peoria, Arizona. She has also been nominated for the Goodreads Choice and RWA Rita Awards. She is the author of several young and new adult romances, including bestsellers Waiting on the Sidelines, The Hard Count, A Boy Like You, This Is Falling and Wild Reckless.

A sucker for a good romance, Ginger's other passion is sports, and she often blends the two in her stories. When she's not writing, the odds are high that she's somewhere near a baseball diamond, either watching her son swing for the fences or cheering on her favorite baseball team, the Arizona Diamondbacks. Ginger lives in Arizona and is married to her college sweetheart whom she met at ASU (fork 'em, Devils).

FIND GINGER ONLINE: www.littlemisswrite.com

facebook.com/GingerScottAuthor

instagram.com/authorgingerscott

tiktok.com/@authorgingerscott